Luca bent toward her, diminutive as she was to his own lean six-two. "What is it that suddenly interests you about me, Sophia? Have you finally decided you need another orgasm to sustain you for the next decade?"

Flames scorched her skin, that was how hot she felt. *Yes* floated to her lips, as if every cell in her had conspired to form that word without her permission. This was easy for him, too easy—riling her up, sinking under her skin. Even knowing what he was, still she reacted like a moth ventured to a flame. "Not everything has to have a sexual connotation in life."

He made to speak, but before he could she covered his mouth with her hand. Long, elegant fingers traced the tender skin of her wrists, leaving brands on her sensitive flesh. The center of her palm burned with the heat of his mouth. Slowly, as if savoring every second of touching her, he pulled her hand from his mouth. Of course, life itself was a big joke to be enjoyed for Luca Conti.

"What did you think I was going to say, Sophia?"

She pursed her mouth tight and took a deep breath. "I have a proposal I'd like to make to you, one that is mutually beneficial to us both."

"There is nothing that you can offer me—" his gaze flicked over her, dismissal and insult all wrapped in those few seconds "—that I won't get from another woman with a whisper, ̶S̶o̶p̶h̶i̶a̶.̶ ̶N̶o̶t̶ tempting."

"You haven't even hea̶[r̶d̶]̶"

"Not interested—"

"I want to marry you."

Tara Pammi

THE UNWANTED
CONTI BRIDE

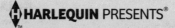

Recycling programs
for this product may
not exist in your area.

ISBN-13: 978-0-373-13452-6

The Unwanted Conti Bride

First North American Publication 2016

Copyright © 2016 by Tara Pammi

Printed in U.S.A.

Tara Pammi can't remember a moment when she wasn't lost in a book—especially a romance, which was much more exciting than a mathematics textbook at school. Years later, Tara's wild imagination and love for the written word revealed what she really wanted to do. Now she pairs alpha males who think they know everything with strong women who knock that theory *and* them off their feet!

Books by Tara Pammi

Harlequin Presents

The Sheikh's Pregnant Prisoner
The Man to Be Reckoned With
A Deal with Demakis

The Legendary Conti Brothers

The Surpise Conti Child

Greek Tycoons Tamed

Claimed for His Duty
Bought for Her Innocence

Society Weddings

The Sicilian's Surprise Wife

A Dynasty of Sand and Scandal

The Last Prince of Dahaar
The True King of Dahaar

The Sensational Stanton Sisters

A Hint of Scandal
A Touch of Temptation

Visit the Author Profile page at Harlequin.com for more titles.

CHAPTER ONE

TONIGHT, SOPHIA ROSSI decided with mounting desperation, her spirit animal would be a skunk.

Because desperation had a particularly pungent stink. It probably clung to her pores, spraying whiffs of it over pitying and curious bystanders, betraying her panic.

She had never belonged in the uber-rich Milanese society that her stepfather and mother dwelled in, was only a Rossi because Salvatore had adopted her after marrying her mother when Sophia had been thirteen. Facts of her life she'd never been allowed to forget by the crowd around her.

She'd somehow weathered the end of her engagement to Leandro Conti.

But this latest rumor—her supposed affair with her one real friend, Kairos Constantinou, who was Leandro's sister's new husband—had made her an object of gossip and even malice. If she'd known what a spectacle it made of her, she'd have refused Leandro's invite to his brother Luca's birthday party, which had been extended weeks ago. The invite was only driven by his guilt at breaking their engagement.

Her fingers tightening over the fragile champagne flute, she made a casual, painted-smile-in-place round around the curving, wide balcony of the Villa de Conti.

Somehow they'd made her into this temperamental shrew, this marriage-wrecking wanton that had become a liability to her family rather than an asset.

How had she, despite all her hard work, jeopardized the most important goal of her life—to support her stepfather, Salvatore, and rebuild Rossi Leather until her half brothers were old enough to take over?

Antonio Conti, the patriarch of the Conti family, reached her just as Sophia deflected another barbed insult. Glassy and brittle it might be, but she didn't let the smile drop from her face.

Silver threaded abundantly through his black hair. Antonio reminded her of a wolf—cunning, wily and quick to gobble up unsuspecting prey.

"Tell me, Sophia," he said, neatly cornering her near a white pillar, "whose idea was it to propose a marriage between my grandson and you?"

Swallowing her shock, Sophia stared at him. No one should have even guessed. "Our engagement is irrelevant now that Leandro is married."

"Your stepfather is ambitious but not clever," Antonio continued as if Sophia hadn't even spoken. "Hardworking but no vision. Even knowing of my desperation to find a bride for my grandsons, Salvatore would have never thought to offer you.

"He has no use for women."

The words were curt, even cruel in their efficient summation. But true.

Sophia had been trying for a decade to get Sal to see the value she could provide for the company, with zero progress. He gave her small projects, refused to listen to her ideas for Rossi Leather.

All he cared about was leaving a legacy for her half brothers, Bruno and Carlo.

"It was mine," she admitted. What did she have to lose at this point? "There was advantage to your family and mine in that match."

Sal could hold grudges on Leandro Conti and the Conti family for breaking the engagement, but Sophia was nothing if not practical.

Rossi Leather couldn't tide over their latest financial setback by alienating the powerful Contis. Antonio still held much sway over the older generation in the leather industry and Leandro Conti, his eldest grandson and CEO of Conti Luxury Goods, held the younger, more heated generation.

Antonio's second grandson, Luca Conti, however... had no clout or morals. Probably no talent. Just oodles of charm, sexuality and utter self-indulgence.

Even thinking about him made her cross. And bitter. And her knees weak.

She'd spent nights pacing her bedroom, sleepless, panicky, when the idea of marrying Leandro had presented itself to her. She'd made herself sick. She'd had nightmares about her past and present morphing into a distasteful, torturous future.

But the welfare of her family had precedence over naive decade-old dreams.

Antonio didn't look surprised. But then he'd known

to ask that question, hadn't he? His silvery brows rose. "You're a curiously resourceful young woman, Sophia."

Sophia's cheeks heated up. "Even for a half-Italian bastard girl with a broken engagement behind her, you mean?"

He continued looking at her.

If she hadn't lost her finer sensibilities a long time ago, if she hadn't developed elephant-thick skin, she'd have been insulted by the purely assessing look the old man cast her, from the top of her dark hair in an efficient knot to the soles of her black Conti pumps, her only nod to fashion, with leisurely stops at her face and several other areas of her body.

"I'm not a cow to be assessed," she added with a glare. The flash of something in his gaze gave her the creeps. "I'm not in the market for an alliance anymore, either." There was only so much she could stomach, apparently, even for her family. "Of any kind," she added for good measure.

Amusement shifted the rigid lines of his face. Flashes of a similar set of features sent a flutter down her spine. "You're not only dedicated to your family but you're also sharp and fearless. I like you, Sophia."

Rarely did the opposite sex, except for her ten-year old brothers, say something that wasn't condescending or insulting to her. "I wish I could say the same. But I've seen you use everyone's shortcomings to your own advantage, including Sal's."

His smile lingered. "Then why not advise your stepfather?"

She remained silent, frustration a quiet snarl inside her. Because Sal never listened to her. He loved her, but not enough to trust her judgment or intelligence when it came to Rossi Leather. All of which she was aware the cunning wolf knew.

"I can give you a way to help Salvatore, Sophia. Without throwing yourself at a married man."

Stinging anger burned Sophia's cheeks but she stayed still. He'd baited her well and he knew it. She was going to throttle whoever had started that distasteful rumor.

"I will pour capital into Salvatore's business," Antonio continued, "create new contracts for him, bring him back into the old class, so to speak. After his string of poor business decisions, he certainly needs the help."

"I'm not for sale," Sophia retorted, a slow panic building inside. She felt like a donkey with a carrot visible but just out of reach. "I suggested marriage to Leandro as a way to help Sal, but I'd have kept every vow I made to him. I would've been a good wife."

"You believe I did not realize that? You believe I would let Salvatore…*persuade* me into letting you marry my grandson without learning all about you? It is exactly why I make this proposal."

Her pulse sped up. "What is your proposal?" she forced herself to say.

"I do have another grandson, *si*? Bring Luca to the altar, marry him and I will take a firm handle on Rossi financial matters. Your mother, your brothers, their futures will never be in peril."

"No!" Her sharp reply turned heads toward them.
Marry Luca, the Conti Devil?

The very idea was like walking on shards of glass
for the rest of her life. *Bare feet and with a lead weight
over her head.* "I don't want to spend an evening with
the Conti Devil, much less marry him."

As though invoked by their discussion, Luca Conti
appeared in the midst of the perfectly manicured lawn
before them, a tall, gorgeous blonde following him like
a faithful puppy.

A woman on his arm, as always.

The rage in those languid, smoky eyes the night of
her engagement to his brother had haunted her. But
he'd avoided her as she'd done for a decade.

His dark, wavy hair was in that same stylish cut.
Low on the sides and piled high on his head, making
his angular face even narrower. Sophistication and
grace oozed from his every stride. But any kind of
austerity ended with his hair.

Because Luca Conti was the most beautiful man
she'd ever seen.

His face, now visible only in flashes as he moved
through the crowd with that loose-limbed stride had
such perfect lines that her breath caught even from
this distance.

Broad shoulders lovingly hugged by gray silk, nar-
rowing to a tapered waist and muscular thighs honed
to pure steel by hours and hours of swimming. He
moved sinuously through the crowd, the tall woman
a beautiful accessory around his lean and wiry body,
a little on the thin side.

But who could remember all that after one glance at his face?

Wide-set, jet-black eyes, with dark blue smudges underneath, always the shadows underneath his eyes as if the man never slept, a steel blade of a nose and a wide mouth made of plump, lush lips that invited one, two…oh, a hundred glances.

Collagen had nothing on this man's mouth…

A mouth that invited sin with one word… A mouth he knew how to use every which way…

Sharp cheekbones created planes and grooves, in concert with the high forehead, as if every inch of it had been painstakingly designed and carved to render him breathtaking.

Those features should have been effeminate, too beautiful, yet something in his gaze, in his will, immediately imposed his fierce masculinity on the onlooker, as if the space around him had to become an extension of him.

And the devil was aware of his exquisite beauty, and the effect it had on the female sex, whether they were seventeen or seventy.

It was clear, from even up there, that Luca was sloshed if not drunk and so was the disreputable beauty, who also happened to be the Italian Finance minister's *almost* ex-wife, Mariana.

Had she thrown away her powerful husband for Luca? Did she know that Luca would dispose of her like a toddler did last week's toys?

Sophia could almost, *only almost*, feel pity for the woman.

The hiss of a curse falling from Antonio's mouth by her side punctured her obsessively greedy perusal.

Luca, as usual, was creating a ruckus. Heads turned toward him, including Kairos and Valentina. A stiff-lipped Leandro cast a hand on Luca to stop him but his younger brother pushed it away.

Whispers abounded, like the drone of insects.

As indulgent as his family and friends were of his usual escapades, it seemed an open lovers' spat—for Luca and the lady's argument was becoming clear now—with another man's wife was too scandalous for them to overlook.

"This is the man you want me to wed? The man who shamelessly shows off his affair with another man's wife with no thought to his family or hers? The man who thinks every woman is a challenge to be conquered, a bet to win?" The memory of her own humiliation at his hands was like acid in her throat. "One who tramples hearts like they were little pieces of glass? I wouldn't touch Luca if he were the last man on earth."

Antonio turned toward her slowly, as if that small movement cost him a great effort. One look into his eyes and Sophia knew he was going in for the kill. Now she was the deer caught in the wolf's sights.

"Are you aware, Sophia, that the bank is ready to call Salvatore's loan in? Or that he has no way to meet the next production per schedule?"

Her heart sank to her toes. "That's not true. He applied for an extension—"

"And was denied."

Sunken eyes peered at her with a cunning that sent chills down her spine. He'd done this, she knew.

Oh, Salvatore had paved the way to their financial ruin with his own faulty decisions but this latest setback—the bank's refusal for an extension—was Antonio's doing.

Apparently, Antonio was just as desperate as she was. "Even if I were to agree to your outrageous proposal—" her entire life tied to that reckless play-boy who had made her so weak once "—how do you think I can accomplish this? Even I, desperate that I am, can't drag a man to the altar. And definitely not the Conti Devil, who cares for nothing except his own pursuits."

Drunk as he was, Luca had somehow managed to steer the clinging woman away from the crowd. But her husky laughter and frantic begging in Italian could be heard from where they were standing, behind and beneath the balcony.

Heat tightened Sophia's cheeks as she understood the gist of the woman's phrases in Italian. Instead of distaste and fury, she felt pity.

The woman was in love with Luca.

Antonio dragged his gaze away from Luca, his mouth a tight line. His frail body seemed to vibrate with distaste, rage and, Sophia sensed with mounting shock, grief. Antonio Conti was grief-stricken over his grandson Luca. *Why?*

The image of the manipulative old man shifted in her mind, even as he took a deep breath, as if to push away the emotion. "No, my grandson cares for nothing in this world. His parents are long dead and Leandro, too, has washed his hands of Luca now.

"But to protect Valentina and her happiness, Luca will do anything. He will make a bargain with anyone to keep her birth a secret from the world."

Sophia gasped, unable to believe what she was hearing. "Her birth? This is not right. I want no part of it—"

"Valentina is not my son's daughter. She is the product of an affair their mother had with her driver. And if this comes out, it will ruin Valentina's standing in society and even her marriage to your friend Kairos.

"So use it to bind Luca to you. He will bend for Valentina's happiness."

No words came to her as Sophia stared at Antonio.

The idea of blackmailing the Conti Devil didn't bother her so much as using Valentina's secret. Dear God, she didn't want to hurt anyone.

An acidic taste lingered in her mouth. "There are too many innocent people involved in this. I won't hurt one of them just because—"

"Just because Salvatore might lose the company? Just because your mother and brothers might have to leave their estate, give up their cars, their place in this society? And what will you do, Sophia? Take up the project manager job your Greek friend offers you to support them? Quietly stand by as Salvatore watches chunks of his company broken down and auctioned off?"

"Why me? Why can't you find a willing woman and force *him* to marry her? Why—"

"Because you're tough and you do what needs to be done. You don't have silly ideas of love in your head. Only you will do for the Conti Devil."

Only you...

Antonio Conti's words reverberated through Sophia.

Oh, how she wished she'd not come tonight... Now she had a possible way to dig their finances out of the ruin but it would only be achieved by selling her soul to the devil...

She wasn't considering it, Sophia told herself, as she walked through the unending corridor of Villa de Conti. The black-and-white-checkered floor gave the mounting nausea within a physical bent.

Surely Antonio deluded himself that his devil-may-care, womanizing grandson could care about his sister. But she had to try. She had to see if there was a chance of salvaging their finances, if there was even a small sliver of hope that her mother, Salvatore and the twins wouldn't be driven to the road.

She reached a wide, circular veranda at the back of the villa.

Jacket discarded, shirt open to reveal a dark olive chest, cuffs folded back, Luca stood leaning against the wall. A foot propped up against it, eyes closed, face turned to the sky. The curving shadows his long eyelashes cast on his cheekbones were like scythes.

Scythes and blades. Her usually nonviolent thoughts revolved around weapons when it came to Luca.

Moonlight caressed the planes of his face, shadows

diluting the magnificent symmetry of his features. Rendering him a little less gorgeous.

A little less captivating.

A little less devilish.

Almost vulnerable and…strangely lonely.

Slowly, Sophia became aware of her own reaction. Damp palms. Skittering heartbeat. Pit in her stomach. Even after a decade, her body went into some kind of meltdown mode near him.

She must have made a sound because his eyes opened slowly. Only his eyes were visible in the silvery light. They fell on her, widened for an infinitesimal fraction of a second, searched her face and then assumed that laid-back, casual, infuriatingly annoying expression that she hated.

"Sophia Rossi, of steel balls and tough skin and icy heart." Whatever alcohol he'd imbibed, his speech didn't slur. Mocking and precise, it arrowed past her defenses. "Did you lose your way, *cara*?"

His sultry voice thickened the air around them so much that Sophia wondered if she could breathe through it. "Stop calling me…" No, that was way too personal. If she was going to do this, Sophia had to enclose herself in steel, lock away even the slightest vulnerability she had, not that she had any. She'd do this for her family, but she wasn't going to be the Conti Devil's amusement. Not this time.

He pushed himself from the wall while she formed and disposed words. When she looked up again, he'd moved close enough for her to smell the crisply masculine scent of him. The light from the hall caressed his features.

Breath was lost. Nerves fluttered. A sigh built and ballooned inside her chest. That small scar under his chin. The sweeping arch of his eyebrows. The razor-sharp lines of his cheekbones. Darkly angelic features that masked a cruel devil.

Jet-black eyes glinted with sardonic amusement at her mute appraisal. He propped a bent hand on the wall she was leaning against, sticking his other hip out. A pose full of grace and languor. Of feigned interest and wretched playfulness. "Tell me, how did you end up in the farthest reaches of the house, away from all the wheelings and dealings of your business friends? Did Little Bo Peep lose track of her sheep and wander into big bad wolf's way?"

Sophia tried to command every cell in her body to keep it together, wrenched herself into a tight ball so that all that touched her was the man's whispery breath. "You're getting your fairy tales mixed up."

"But my point got through to you, *si*?" He ran the heel of his hand over his tired-looking eyes while Sophia stared hungrily, cataloging every gesture, every shift. "What do you want, Sophia?"

"Your...*situation* looked like it needed rescuing."

The slight tug of his mouth transformed into that full-blown grin that always seemed to be waiting for an invite. Evenly set teeth gleamed in an altogether wicked face. "Ahh...and so Sophia Rossi, the righteous and the pure, decided to come to my aid."

"Where is your lover? I can have one of our chauffeurs drive her home."

His gaze held hers, a thousand whispers in it. "She's in my bed, thoroughly lost to the world." It dipped to her mouth. Snaky tendrils of heat erupted over her skin. "I believe I wore her out."

Nausea hit Sophia with the force of a gardening hose, the images of a sweaty and ravished Mariana burning her retinas as if she could see the leggy blonde amidst a cloud of soft, white sheets.

Luca's bedroom—pure white sheets, gleaming black marble, black-and-white portraits all around... It was like being transported into your worst nightmare and your darkest fantasy, all rolled into one. While being naked and blindfolded and without any defense.

She let all the disgust she felt seep to the surface and stepped back.

"Don't you think this is too far even for you? They are not even divorced yet. And you're advertising it for all and sundry to see."

"But that's the fun, *si*? Tangling with the dangerous? Riling up her husband into one of his awful tempers?"

"And then you walk away?" *Like you did from me.* "Her life will be in ruins in terms of the society, while you latch on to the next willing v—"

His mouth curved into a snarl and his hand covered her mouth. Opal fire burned in his eyes. "Is that what you tell yourself, *cara*? That you were a victim all those years ago? Have you convinced yourself that I forced you?"

She pushed away his hand and glared at him, all the while pretending that her lips still didn't tingle from the heat of his touch. That she didn't burn at the memory… "I didn't mean that you take them without their… Damn it, Luca, you and I both know he will ruin her over this."

"Maybe ruin is exactly what Mariana wants. Maybe to be utterly debauched by me is her only salvation." The words were silky, casual, and yet…for the first time in her life, Sophia saw more than the hauntingly beautiful face, the wicked grin, even the seductive charm. "You would not understand her, Sophia."

"I just don't think—"

Sophia watched that lazy face swallow away that fury, saw the emotion blank out of his eyes as easily as if someone had taken an eraser and wiped it away. "I don't give a damn about your opinions, so, *per carita*, stop expressing them." He bent toward her, diminutive as she was to his own lean six-two. "What is it that suddenly interests you about me, Sophia? Have you finally decided you need another orgasm to sustain you for the next decade?"

Flames scorched her skin; that was how hot she felt. *Yes* floated to her lips, as if every cell in her had conspired to form that word without her permission.

This was easy for him, too easy—riling her up, sinking under her skin. Even knowing what he was, still she reacted like a moth venturing to a flame. "Not everything has to have a sexual connotation in life."

"Says the woman who needs to be utterly and thoroughly—"

This time her hand clamped his mouth. Sophia glared at him. His breath kissed her sensitive palm.

Long, elegant fingers traced the tender skin of her wrists, leaving brands on her sensitive flesh. Slowly, as if savoring every second of touching her, he pulled her hand. "What did you think I was going to say, Sophia?"

She pursed her mouth and took a deep breath. "I have a proposal I'd like to make to you, one that is mutually beneficial."

"There is nothing that you can offer me—" his gaze flicked over her, dismissal and insult in that look "—that I won't get from another woman, Sophia."

"You haven't even heard it."

"Not interested—"

"I want to marry you."

CHAPTER TWO

Not "will you marry me, Luca?"

Not "I think it makes sense for me to marry you now even though I've hated you for a decade and chose your brother over you just a few months ago."

Not "I need you to save my stepfather from sure financial ruin, so, *please, oh, please*, won't you make me your wife?"

No, Sophia Rossi proposed marriage as she did everything else.

Like a charging bull and with the confidence that she could bend, twist or generally command him into doing her bidding. Probably with an adoring smile on his face, and the marble digging into his knees if she could manage it.

Dio, where did the woman's strength come from?

Luca Conti swallowed his astonishment. Her loyalty in considering this for her family's sake, when he knew how much she hated him—and with good reason—was admirable. He ignored the thudding slam of his heart against his rib cage—she was a weakness and a regret he'd never quite forgotten—and gave free rein to the riding emotion.

Amusement. Sheer hilarity.

It burst out of him like an engulfing wave of the ocean, like a rising crescendo of music, punching the air out of his throat with its force. There was a knot in his gut. Hand shaking, he wiped his wet cheeks.

What merciful God had granted him this wonderful moment?

For reasons all too Freudian, Luca hated his birthday. Loathed, despised with the hatred of a thousand exploding supernovas. But his self-loathing, as brightly as it flared from time to time, to his brother Leandro's eternal gratitude, had never overtaken his respect for life.

Over the years he had become better at handling his birthday. There was even a memorable threesome sprinkled through a couple of them. But not one of those miserable thirty birthdays had presented him with a gift like this one.

Just months ago Sophia had chosen Leandro over him to marry.

To see the one woman he had given up years ago—granted, after thoroughly breaking her heart—as his brother's wife every day would have been the straw that broke the camel's back. In other words, destination Hell on a direct flight.

He would have had to let the engagement go forward. The wedding itself, probably not.

He'd have seduced her, for sure. He'd have had to do it before the wedding, he remembered telling himself in a drunken haze. Luckily, his—now—sister-in-law Alex had shown up, turned Leandro's life inside out and spun Luca away from that necessary but destructive course.

And here Sophia was now…proposing marriage to *him* this time. The woman had balls. He loved her for that if nothing else. "I believe this is the best birthday present I've ever received, *bella*. How the mighty fall. Wait till I—"

He heard the outraged snarl before a filthy word fell from her stiff-lined mouth, and it was like a violin had joined the piano in his head. "If you tell anyone, I'll cut off—"

He burst out laughing again.

"Go to hell," she whispered, her petite frame radiating fury. Most of it self-directed, he knew, for Sophia hated betraying any emotion that made her weak.

He caught her wrist and pulled her inside the large, and thankfully empty, lounge behind them. Backing her into the wall, he pulled her arms above her.

The disdain in her eyes, the arrogant jut of her chin… It was like pouring petrol over a spark. Jerked at every primal instinct he had carefully banished from his life. Her breasts heaved as she fought him, as if they too fought against being confined.

"You thought you would propose marriage and walk away? You did not think I would find it entertaining?"

"You're a remorseless bastard." It was the first time she'd hinted at their past.

Regret was a faint pang in Luca's chest. Only faint.

Did he regret that he had hurt her ten years ago? *Si.*

So much that if given the chance he wouldn't do it again? *Non.*

He was far too selfish to willingly deny himself the true joy he'd found with her in those few weeks. "And you love playing the uptight shrew far too much."

Outrage, and most improbably, hurt, transformed her muddy brown eyes into a thousand hues of golds and bronzes.

Her stubborn, too-prominent nose flared. Incongruously wide mouth in a small face flushed a deep pink. The hourglass figure swathed in the most horrific black dress rubbed against him, bringing him to painful arousal.

In front of his eyes, she became something else.

She became the Sophia he'd known once and hadn't been able to resist, the Sophia he'd kissed with wonder, the Sophia she'd been before he had beat all the softness out of her.

She grunted and gave herself away, seconds before she raised her knee to his groin.

"How would this marriage of ours…*prosper and proliferate* if you turn me into a castrato, Sophia?"

Dancing his lower body away from her kick, he used the momentum to slam her harder into his hip. Her soft belly pressed and flushed into the lines of his body, his hip bone digging into it, as if it meant to make a groove for itself against her.

A softer gasp escaped her this time, throaty and wrenched away from the part of her she hid so well. So well that he had often wondered if he had known her so intimately once. That short huff for breath stroked Luca's nerves. Like strings of a violin…

Thick, wavy locks of hair fell from the ugly knot

at the back of her head, touching the strong planes of her face with softness. The floral scent of her shampoo, something so incongruous with the woman she was, *or pretended to be*, fluttered under his nose. Luca pressed his nose into the thick, wavy mass. Kneaded the tense planes of her upper back as if he could calm himself by calming her.

He had never forgotten his amazement at the fire that had flared between them, how easily his plan had gone utterly wrong ten years ago. How, even for his jaded palate, Sophia had proved to be too much of a temptation.

Dio, suggesting marriage to him, of all men... Hadn't she learned her lesson? Why was she tempting the devil in him?

He *was* tempted. What man wouldn't want to muss up those ugly dresses and that shrewish facade and want to find the soft woman beneath? What man wouldn't want a claim on that kind of loyalty, on that steely core of her?

He set her away from him, none too gently. Lust riding him hard, he drew one rattling breath after another.

He controlled the pursuit of pleasure and the pleasure itself. Without shame or scruples, he used his charm, his looks, to draw women to him, amused himself for a time and then walked away.

He'd carefully built his life to be that and nothing more. He'd trampled her innocence even when he'd intended to do the right thing once. But in the end, he'd left. He would walk away again.

After having a small taste. She really expected it

of him—to behave abominably, to torture her with his lascivious words and deeds. He couldn't disappoint her.

His humor restored, he eased his grip on her. Instantly she shoved at him. He didn't budge. "I can think of an infinitely more pleasurable *and* mature way to vent your frustration."

"It's hard to be mature when you laugh in my face like this."

"Your dignity is that fragile? The Sophia I keep hearing about in boardrooms and business mergers is apparently nothing short of Goddess Diana."

He curved his mouth into his trademark smile. Her glare didn't dim one bit. If anything, she stiffened even more.

Dio, when was the last time he had had such fun? And they hadn't even shed their clothes yet. "I was right, it is I that gets under your skin."

Her eyelids fell slowly. A second to restore her quaking defenses. Right on cue, she looked up, her fiery glare renewed. "I forgot that it's all a big joke to you."

"Being a debauched playboy who cares for nothing is hard work."

"I was stupid to think we could have a mature conversation. All you—"

"Then persuade me."

"What?"

Surprise in her gaze filled him with a strange satisfaction. Shocking, needling, generally startling Sophia out of that hard shell could become addictive. "Persuade me. Indulge me. Make me an irresistible offer."

* * *

Make herself irresistible to the most beautiful man on the face of the planet? A man who held nothing sacred?

"I have a better chance of finding treasure in my backyard," she said softly. Wistfulness snuck into her voice and she cringed.

"Kiss me, then."

"What?" She rubbed her temples, dismayed at how he reduced her to a mumbling idiot.

"Put your lips on mine and pucker them up. Your hands can go on my shoulders or my hips or if you're feeling bold, you can grab my ass—"

"What? Why?" Years of oratory at debate club evaporated, her brain only offering whats and whys.

"That should be the first step for a couple considering marriage, *si*? I could never marry a woman who didn't know how to kiss."

Don't. Look. At. His. Mouth. "It's obvious you're only torturing me and will never really consider it and you…" She looked and the contoured lushness of it made her lick her own lips, which made him grin and prompted her to raise her gaze. "Your lover is lying in your bed and you're—"

"If you'd been paying attention and not mooning over me—" Sophia fisted her hands, just fighting the urge to wipe that satisfied smile off his face, for he was right, damned devil "—then you would know that Mariana and I are over."

"You just said you wore her out!" Her brow cleared. "You said that just to rile me up, didn't you? There was hardly any time between when you left and I found

you for you to…to—" She couldn't believe what her logic led her to say. If only she could stop blushing! "—*wear her out*."

"I actually don't need that much time to get my lover off—"

"Where is she?" Sophia cut him off.

"She's a lightweight and I kept plying her with drinks. Her husband's divorcing her, which is what she wanted, but she's a little emotional about it. I couldn't just…throw her out of the party when she was in such a state."

"No, of course not. They all adore you even when you're done with them."

Except her, Luca thought with something akin to a pang in his chest.

"You're free to adore me, too, *cara*. No one will have to know."

She snorted. That inelegant movement of that sharp, stubborn nose made him chuckle. "*God*, really, you don't need any more admirers, secret or otherwise. *And* I'm not kissing you."

Pink and wide, her mouth was like a long bow, the only feature in her face that was soft and vulnerable. A pillow of lushness. It betrayed that tough-as-nails, no-nonsense persona of hers.

He desperately wanted to feel it under his own, wanted to taste all that pent-up passion. One kiss wouldn't hurt. She was the one who'd cornered him, the one throwing outrageous ideas at him, the one looking all delectably confined and uptight in that dress. "How do you expect me to believe you're not playing a joke on me with this proposal? Maybe this is revenge? Maybe you intend to make me fall in love with you, and then leave me at the altar pining for you? Maybe..."

Brown eyes glittering, wide mouth mobile, she laughed. It was a full-throttled laugh, deep and husky. The kind that came all the way from your stomach, burned through your lungs, leaving you a little dizzy. Her body shook all over.

The sound stole into Luca, filling every hungry crevice inside him. It was one that could cut through the darkest space, filling it with light. "What is so funny?"

"You, falling in love. *With me.*"

He said it softly. "The whole world assumes Sophia Rossi is tough, brave, the conqueror of every challenge. Decimator of men. Only I know what a coward you are."

It fell in the space between them like a weapon, and he waited, breath balling up in his lungs. Anger and apprehension vied in her face until she covered the distance between them. He didn't know if she was going to slap him or kiss him or castrate him. No woman could create that mystery except Sophia. No woman had ever filled his veins with this heady anticipation.

Fingers on the lapels of his shirt, she jerked him close. "No one calls me a coward, *you manipulative bastard.*"

Throaty and tart, growly and yet with a deep vein of need pulsing beneath, it was Sophia to the end.

Brave Sophia accepting facts and meeting them head-on. Dutiful Sophia kissing the man she hated just to hear him out.

Short and curvy, she barely came up to his chest. Hands on his shoulders, she pulled herself up, as if to elongate herself. Like a vine clinging to a cement wall.

That pressed every inch of her to him. Lush breasts, followed by such a thin waist that he wondered how it held up those glorious curves, then flaring into rounded hips, hips a man would anchor himself on while he thrust inside her. Shapely thighs that would clutch a man tight as he jerked in pleasure within her velvet heat.

Again and again, until he forgot what or who he was.

Such heat rolled over his skin that Luca's fingers dug into her soft flesh.

With a protesting moan, she stilled her mouth on his. The tips of their noses collided and a soft sigh left her. Hot breath kissed his hungry lips. Then she moved that mouth again. Testing and trying. This way and that. Halting thoughtfully and then hurrying along urgently when she liked the fit.

Brown eyes met his. And the world stilled. Time and space narrowed to this minute, this space around them. Never breaking his gaze, she slanted her head and dragged a kiss from one corner of his mouth to the other.

She took control of the kiss like she did everything else.

And Luca let her take over. Let the scent and taste

of her fill every hungry crevice. Let her imprint herself on him.

Flames of fire raced along his veins when she licked the seam of his lips and probed for entry. Desperate, Luca opened his mouth under hers. The throaty sound of her gasp shivered down his spine. Never had he been waiting like this for pleasure. Never had he been the recipient.

Suppressing every instinct to take over the reins of the kiss—he'd never waited to be pleasured—he let her seduce him. She obliged, stroking the inside of his mouth with bold flicks, teasing and incinerating. Took his mouth with a carnality that left him shaking to the very marrow.

Christo, he'd never been so aroused by just a kiss.

The sound of footsteps behind them brought Sophia back to earth with a thud.

Her mouth stung with the taste of Luca, her body thrumming with unsatisfied desire. The crisp hair on his wrists teased her palms.

But she felt anything but exultant. She wanted to cry. She wanted to ask him to take her to his bedroom, turn off the lights and—no, not his bedroom. Not the place where he'd probably made love to a horde of lovers, each more stunning and thin and wispier than the next. Maybe they could slip away into that veranda, hide under the moonlight and he could kiss her a little more.

She could pretend that he'd never broken her heart and that he wanted her just as much as she did him.

Because when Luca kissed her, Sophia was always carried off to some faraway land. A land where she could be strong enough to be weak, where she could let someone care for her, where she didn't worry about her family, where she was not mocked for who she was.

Where a man like Luca didn't have to be induced into seducing a woman like her...

She hid her face in his chest. His heartbeat thundered against her cheek. He was warm and male, both exciting and comforting, something she hadn't realized until this moment she missed.

Sophia couldn't dredge up anger for that kiss. Toward him or herself.

His fingers wandered up and down her hips, questing and caressing. "I'd rather we kissed again, but I keep my word." Deep and hoarse, his voice pinged over her heated skin. "So tell me, why do you wish to…"

Suddenly, a hand on her shoulder pulled her from his arms, turned her around.

"Tina, *non*!" she heard Luca shout dimly.

Sophia didn't see it coming. Someone slapped her. Hard.

Her head went back, pain radiating up her jaw and through her ear. Tears blurred her vision and she blinked to clear them away. Pulling in a shuddering breath, she looked up.

Valentina—Luca's sister and Kairos's wife, stood before her, her lithe, willowy body shaking with rage. Her entire face was mobile with emotion, turning her into a volatile beauty. "You…*you tart*!"

Sophia raised a brow, refusing to show her dismay. "Tart, really?"

Her composure seemed to only rile the younger woman more. "You're determined to go through all the men in my family, aren't you? First Kairos, and now Luca? And to think I felt sorry for you when Leandro broke your engagement."

"Basta, Tina!" Luca again. His arm around Sophia's shoulders, he was a wall of lean strength against her. A dark scowl framed his features, his fingers rubbing against her arm in unconscious comfort.

Against every rational warning, Sophia felt her body leaning into his.

"You know the rumors about Kairos and her?" Tina screeched, her eyes filling with tears.

"If there's truth to them, confront your husband, Tina."

"Fall into her clutches, then. Maybe she will leave my husband alone." Her black gaze raked over Sophia in a sneer. "Although I do not see the appeal."

Valentina left with the same fierceness as she had come in. Like a storm, leaving a minefield of awkward silence behind.

Sophia untangled herself from Luca's side and ran her fingers tentatively over her cheek. She thought she might be a little sick but it could be because of how much dessert she'd eaten in her anxiety tonight after the strict diet of the last two weeks.

Luca pulled her to him; she tried to swat him away.

He won in the fight for possession of her. She swallowed hard. Fingers on her chin, he examined her cheek. "I apologize. She had no right to behave like that." His mouth became a hard line. All the charm, the wicked laughter, was gone.

She waited for the inevitable question about her and Kairos, but it never came. But then, the one thing Luca had never been was a hypocrite.

"Marriage to Kairos is not good for her."

She frowned but he didn't elaborate. "Kairos can be hard to—" he raised a brow and she realized she'd jumped to her supposed lover's defense "—understand."

"You feel sorry for her?" he said, amazement in his eyes.

Sophia shrugged. Despite the sting in her cheek and the burn in her stomach at the comment on her looks, something inside Sophia recoiled at the vulnerability in Valentina's eyes. A palette of emotions for Kairos, who was as hard-hearted as hell, to see. And everything was acted upon, too...

No man was worth that self-doubt, that haunting sense of inadequacy, Sophia wanted to tell Valentina.

Swift anger rose through her at Kairos; he was supposed to be her friend. Couldn't he have reassured Valentina instead of using Sophia to keep his own wife at a distance?

"It's obvious that what I suggested is a disastrous idea." She chanced a glance at Luca, greedy to the last second. She'd make sure it was another decade before she saw him again. Something in her clenched tight. "Forget what I suggested."

Without waiting for his answer, Sophia turned and walked away.

And in that moment she hated all men.

Antonio, for planting that horrible idea in her head, for using her desperation to promote his own agenda.

Kairos, for using their friendship as a barrier against his own wife.

Salvatore, for never giving her a chance in the company, even though he called her his daughter.

And the man behind her, more than anyone else, for kissing her like he meant it. Now and ten years ago. For making her want him so much, for making her weak and foolish, for making her imagine, even for a second, that she was all the things she could never be.

CHAPTER THREE

LUCA SPENT THAT Monday morning with Huang from the design team of Conti Luxury Goods, studying the prototype for new heels that would be released the coming spring.

Huang and he had worked together for almost ten years now, since Leandro had convinced Luca to take a small part in Conti Luxury Goods. Luca interacted only with Huang, and Huang worked with the rest of the design team.

He picked up a royal blue pump, tracing the aerodynamic sole with his fingers. The success of these pieces didn't worry him. As always, anything he designed, from pumps to handbags, became instantly covetous among the fanatically fashionable.

Seeing something raw and shapeless transform into something so pleasing, that was success to him. But this particular design run had come to fruition and he felt the loss of it keenly. It had been quite a challenge— the design of the new heel. Now the production team would take over.

Familiar restlessness slithered through his veins.

What to work on next? Sophia's outrageous proposal from Friday night winked at him.

Dio, but that had challenge and fun and all kinds of things written into it. She hated him—had every right to, but she was still attracted to him. When his looks tripped Sophia into that kind of a kiss, he couldn't quite hate them. It should have been one of a hundred kisses, she one of numerous, interchangeable faces he filled his life with and yet, the taste of her lips lingered, the passion with which she had taken him lingered, filling him with a restless craving for more.

Since he had no intention of following that up with Sophia, he needed a woman. To forget her and her kisses and that he had no place in her life. *Soon.*

He was at the door when Huang said, "You're not going to wait?"

"For what?"

"You don't even know, do you? Your brother—" Huang's smile dimmed for the rift between Leandro and him, the first in their life, was fodder for office gossip "—is at the board meeting today. The one that's going on now."

"Well, he's the CEO of CLG, Huang." His mind ran over the next few days. He couldn't disappear without checking on Tina first.

"There are rumors that he's making a big announcement today."

Luca stilled.

His brother claimed to have changed, that he regretted ruthlessly arranging Tina's marriage to Kairos, pulling such deception over their sister, even if he intended it for her own good. But Leandro did nothing without reason. Needing to control everyone and everything around him was an itch in his brother's blood.

A lot of fates depended on Leandro's decision. Including Salvatore's. And Sophia's.

Her problems are not yours.

No warning could curb his thoughts, though. The poor state of the Rossi finances was common knowledge now. What would be her next move? Who would she propose marriage to next?

Curiosity was wildfire in his gut, eating away at that restlessness that never deserted him. Her expression when she had walked away, defeated yet resolute, stayed with him.

If nothing, it would be amusing to see what Sophia would do next. So Luca waited, for Sophia was a breath of fresh air, cold and yet invigorating, in his predestined life.

Leandro was stepping down as the CEO of the CLG Board.

Two hours and a million thoughts later, Luca still hadn't recovered from the shock. For years Leandro's life had been CLG. Kairos, his brother-in-law, would be the front-runner for CEO.

What use would his sister, Tina,then be to the ruthlessly ambitious Kairos once he had that?

His thoughts in a tangle, Luca walked past the alarmed secretary and pushed the door open to his brother's office.

Kairos was in Leandro's office, his hands on Sophia's shoulders.

Jealousy twisted Luca's gut, his blood singing with that same possessive fury again. *Dio*, only Sophia reduced him to this. Willing control over his emotions, he stayed by the door. The question he'd refused to ask, because he'd believed that Sophia was above such disgusting behavior as him, even after Tina's accusations gnawed at him now.

How well did Sophia know him?

Sophia's quick shake to Kairos's whisper, the intimacy their very stance betrayed…suggested something more than an affair, something far more dangerous.

He couldn't be the only man in the world who realized Sophia's worth, the only man who wanted to claim her in every way. Did Kairos want more, too?

Even if they weren't having an affair, it was clear Sophia had something with Kairos that Tina could never reach.

He'd hated this match between Tina and Kairos from the beginning, but seeing the stars in his sister's eyes, he had stayed out of it. Even now, every instinct in him wanted to let Kairos have the CEO position he'd pursued with such cunning and ruthlessness, to let their marriage reach that destructive conclusion.

Only the tears he'd seen in Tina's eyes at that party stayed his hand now.

It had been Leandro who had brought Tina to live with them after their mother's death but it was Luca who'd made her laugh. Luca who'd gained her trust first; Luca she laughed with over all these years.

With her smile and generous heart, Tina loved Luca unconditionally, provided as much an anchor in his life as Leandro had.

Smarting at the direction of his thoughts, Luca ran a hand through his hair.

If there was a chance that Tina's marriage to Kairos could be saved, he had to take it. He had to trust in Leandro's belief that Kairos was the right man for Tina.

And to give Tina a running chance, he'd take away what stood between his sister and Kairos—the CEO position of CLG and Sophia Rossi. Luca's seat on the board, which he'd have to claim for the first time in his life, would see to the first.

The second…

The solution that appeared released a panic in his gut, as if a noose were tightening around his neck.

Of all the women in the world, Sophia was the last woman he should be contemplating marriage to. She had proved to be dangerous to his peace of mind even as a chubby, composed nineteen-year-old. Now she was a force to be reckoned with.

"Can we borrow…*your office, Kairos*?" Luca interrupted the sweetly nauseating scene. "Sophia and I have something important to discuss."

"I won't let you bully Sophia."

"How about you show that concern for my sister? Your wife, remember?" Luca retorted.

Another squeeze of Sophia's shoulders and Kairos left.

"That looked like a very cozy scene, very tender," Luca said, leaning against the closed door, batting away at the ugly emotion festering in his gut. "I gather he knows what Tina did."

He saw her spine stiffen, making her look like an angry crow in her black dress. "I didn't tell him. And I came by to tell him that he should clear this misunderstanding with Valentina."

As always, the black linen was unadorned with the skirt falling demurely past her knees, high necked and severely cut. Yet the very cut and the way it enfolded all of her emphasized the very voluptuousness of the woman's curves. If her intentions were to cover up that exquisitely luscious body with those painfully severe dresses, then she was an abysmal failure.

The only thing her horribly dowdy dresses showed was her rejection of style and fashion. Of her femininity. That she found herself not worthy enough of even trying.

He wanted to tear the ugly fabric off her and dress her in slithery silks, discover that satiny soft skin that he'd tasted once thoroughly, make her—

"Luca?"

Christo, two minutes in the same room and he could imagine only one scenario. The easy way she unmanned his control made Luca's tone uncharacteristically harsh and bitter. "How did he receive *your mutually beneficial proposal*? Should I be flattered that you asked me first?" Disgustingly shameful words, he realized the moment he spoke.

She stilled, dismay pouring out of her entire frame. That she was hurt by his callous remark, that she could be pushed to some reaction by him, any reaction, elated Luca. *He was truly a twisted devil.*

"No," she said, boldly meeting his eyes, only the shadows in her own betraying her emotions, "you're the only one I've proposed marriage to. And before you ask another disgustingly hypocritical question, no, I've not propositioned Kairos into some sort of illicit affair, either.

"I do not sleep with married men. Much less a close married friend. Much less a man who already asked me to marry him and I refused."

Shock stole coherence from Luca. Suddenly, he saw it.

Ruthlessly ambitious, Kairos had first wanted Sophia and Rossi Leather. When she'd refused, he'd set his sights on Tina and the Conti Board instead, with Leandro's blessing.

And now his dear brother-in-law probably wanted to eat his cake, too…

Dio, now he couldn't undo knowing that Tina's marriage was in trouble.

Sophia hitched her handbag over her shoulder, knuckles white, and glanced at her watch. "If you'll excuse me, I have several other men I have to proposition, blackmail, extort so that I can save my family's livelihood. If you've had enough fun at my expense, I'd like to get started."

"I want to talk about your proposal."

Her hands stilled on her desk. "No." Fury bristled from her. "I used to think you still possessed some notion of decency. But no. You are every horrible thing I thought of you all these years."

"I'm serious, Sophia."

Something shone in her eyes. He'd never met a woman who worked as hard as Sophia did, one who dusted herself off even after being denied every opportunity she deserved.

Such strength, such endurance and yet he knew, like no one else did, that she was vulnerable, too. Was it any wonder she fascinated him?

Sophia stared at Luca, trying to gauge his mood. Trying to banish the taste of him from her mouth.

Even as she knew that she had a better chance of forgetting how to breathe. For a week, she'd lain flushed and restless in her bed, touching her lips, as if she could invoke that feeling again.

Ran a hand over her breasts and down low, where she'd been already damp. Just imagining his fingers down there, his mouth on her heavy breasts, she'd been aching all night. Reaching for something only he could give and she could never ever want again.

Today, he was wearing a V-necked gray sweater and black jeans. With a bristly beard and dark shadows beneath his eyes, he looked exactly the man he was—a recklessly gorgeous playboy with a long night behind him.

"Sophia?"

She came to with a startle, her cheeks on fire. He was serious? He wanted to hear her proposal? "I've heard that Leandro and you are on the outs now?"

"Si." One long finger traced the edge of the desk, and Sophia could tell this was something that bothered him—this rift with his brother.

"With Leandro stepping down, your vote could become the deciding factor on a lot of things."

"Like whether Rossi Leather should be cut for pieces and distributed among everyone."

She nodded, hiding her shock. For a self-indulgent, indolent playboy, Luca grasped the situation far too quickly. "You enjoy the extravagant lifestyle being a Conti affords you. I mean, you're used to those custom designed Armani suits, that flat in downtown Milan, that Maserati and all those women, yes?" she said spitefully, knowing full well that Luca could be a pauper and women would still strip for him in the middle of a birthday party.

He sighed, even as deep amusement glinted in his eyes. "You know I do. I dread losing any of it. I didn't realize Leandro was serious about letting it all go to hell."

"If you give me the required rights, I will do everything Leandro has done for you all these years. Represent you on the board and take care of your interests in CLG. You won't have to lift a finger."

"I see you've used your superior knowledge of my likes and tastes to reel me in." If there was any justice in the world, her glare should have turned him into dust.

"What do you get in return?"

"If we marry, my stepfather could be convinced to bring Rossi's under the umbrella of CLG. He's been resisting it because he thinks his legacy would be swallowed up."

"*Dio*, controlling old men and their obsession with their legacies. So this agenda is not driven by Kairos, then."

"What?"

He shrugged. "You have to admit it's a good theory. Kairos decides you'll marry me, can have me by the balls and consequently, has my vote in his bid to be CEO."

"That is too ruthless even for him. Not forgetting the obvious flaw in the plan that I, of all women, could have your ba—" She gasped; it was like there was her own personal furnace inside her, and the rogue grinned as she cleared her throat. "Could have you under my control, in any manner."

"I could never marry a woman who lacks in feminine wiles."

She gritted her teeth. He had to pick the most uncomfortable aspect of that. "Another fantastic reason for why it's a crazy idea."

He gave her a considering look. "If you have such faith in that bastard Kairos, then why not accept his help?"

"Luca, what is your problem with Kairos?"

"He's too hungry for power. Which means he'll do anything in his hunt for it."

"Yes, how infinitely atrocious that Kairos is so ambitious when he could be chasing woman after woman in eternal pursuit of pleasure."

"Why isn't he helping you with Rossi's?"

"He offered but I don't like his solution. Everyone, including Kairos, has an agenda for Rossi Leather without considering what's actually best for the company or my family. And the problems we have aren't going to be solved by a simple influx of cash. Salvatore will bring us back here into this same situation in a year again. No one can help us."

Not even Antonio.

The minute she didn't toe the line—which would probably include some impossible task like domesticating the devil in front of her—Antonio would tighten the screws on her. Threaten their company or withdraw his support.

"The only way to ensure we don't fall into this hole again," she said, with a mounting sense of defeat, "is if I take the reins myself."

"You think Leandro would have recognized how smart and efficient you are and given you the reins. That's why you were so eager to marry him."

"He always struck me as a fair, principled man."

Her unshakeable trust, the admiration in Leandro's implacable nature, rubbed Luca raw.

He had never bemoaned the fact that only he, and not Leandro, had inherited every despicable thing from their father—his good looks, his brilliance and maybe his madness. But in that moment he envied his brother the freedom to be his own man, the right to his own mind that made Sophia admire him so much.

"You would have married him, shared his bed?" Fury threaded his tone, which shocked her as much as him. "After the history we have?"

Color mounted her cheeks. "Rossi's needs a complete rehaul, five years to build it to a stable position again. Leandro would have given me that chance."

Her stepfather's damned company... It always came back to that. "I've no doubt that you will do it in three. You'll make Rossi's better than it has ever been."

Shock rooted Sophia to the floor, a faint whooshing in her ears making her dizzy. She ran a shaking hand over her brow. "What?"

"*Dio*, you sang this same song even a decade ago. You went into raptures, *non, you almost climaxed* with anticipation every time you talked about your plans for your Rossi Leather. Extension, branching away from leather production completely, focusing on accessory design... Just do it already, Sophia."

He stared at her, brows raised in question while Sophia processed those words slowly. Dear God, he remembered all of her naive, hopeful, detailed plans for Rossi's.

Heat pricked her eyes. Her head hurt as if under some great liquid weight; even her nose felt thick. Or rough. Or something very close to tears.

Did he know what a gift he gave her?

He didn't give the compliment grudgingly like Kairos, who recognized talent and hunted it with a ruthless will. He didn't give the compliment insidiously, as if her intellect and smart business sense were odd, distorting it into some sort of stain on her femininity. As if somehow they minimized her as a woman.

He didn't give it to placate her, like her mother. Even her mother, she knew, wished Sophia was different. Wished *Sophia made it easy on herself*; wished *Sophia didn't feel like she had to prove herself in a man's world.*

Wished *Sophia wasn't still fighting, even after all these years.*

No, Luca stated it as a matter of fact. With the same tone as if to say: people need oxygen to live.

Given the chance, Sophia Rossi could make Rossi's better than it has ever been before.

Simply that.

Just that.

Joy bloomed from her chest, spreading like warm honey through every cell, stretching her mouth into a wide smile.

He came to stand before her, and for once, Sophia couldn't step back. It seemed as if he had thoroughly bypassed all her defense mechanisms. "Sophia?"

"Hmmm?"

"You have a blank look in your eyes, and I'm not sure you've breathed in the last ten seconds. Also... you're smiling at me like I'm your favorite person in the world. *Dio*, you're not dying, are you?" He tilted her chin up, raked her face over with that searing gaze. "Now that I think about it, you look like you've lost weight and there are dark shadows under your eyes."

Her hands drifted to her hips and his gaze followed it eagerly. She pulled them up as if burned. The scent of him stroked over her senses. Just a little dip at her waist and her breasts would graze his chest. Her legs would tangle with his. And then she could—

"This is not some pathetic, last-minute attempt to

have some good sex before you die, is it?" Something glittered in his gaze as he gently ran a finger over her cheek. "Because, *cara mia*, we don't have to marry for that. All you have to do is ask and I will *gladly* show you how fun it is on this side."

When was the last time she'd had fun? "I'm not dying."

"As much as that would solve a lot of problems for me, that is good to know. Now, I will give you three months of marriage."

Sophia couldn't believe he was agreeing to a proposal she'd made in sheer desperation. He seemed to decide as easily as he'd decide which party to go to. *Or which woman to take home on a given night.* Worse, she couldn't believe the way every cell in her leaped at the chance to be near him. Three months as his wife... *Lord*, it was both her salvation *and* utter ruin. "Why are you helping?"

"One, I want to throw a small hitch in my brother-in-law's plans. Two, I hate working, as you neatly pointed out."

Her heart sank to the floor. "You're doing this to drive a wedge between Kairos and me? I told you I'm not sleeping with him."

"A little distance wouldn't hurt, then. Especially if it is provided by me. Leandro has washed his hands of me. I'll have to claim my seat on the board. And like you said, who better than my own wife to watch out for my interests and work in my stead? We both get what we want."

"What is it that you're promising exactly?"

"You can't turn Rossi's around in three months but it's a start in digging it out of that hole, *si*?" He tucked an errant curl behind her cheek, a wicked smile on his mouth. "I want to give you what you want, Sophia. And a couple of things you are too stubborn to ask for."

Her cheeks heated up. If it beat any faster, her heart was going to burst out of her chest. Her gaze lowered to his mouth, cinders lighting up her blood. *Don't. Ask. Don't*—"Your arrogance in yourself is breathtaking."

"Arrogance, *bella mia*? I state fact. You know where you're going to end up."

Memories and sensations rushed through her— rough breaths, the slide of hot, damp skin like velvet over hers, pain giving way to incredible pleasure… every other sense amplified in the darkness that she'd insisted on…

Heat poured through her, like lava spewing out. Her skin felt tight, parched, her pulse ringing through her. "No… I don't want to sleep with you ever again."

"Who mentioned anything about sleep? Just don't fall in love with me," he added with a grin.

"I'm not a naive idiot anymore," Sophia replied, confident that she'd avoid that trap.

Luca was irresistible but she was walking into this with her eyes wide open.

Love wasn't for her; he'd helped her see that first-hand. She'd hated the loss of control over her own happiness, over her mood, over her sense of self-worth. In a moment Luca had stripped her of everything.

She despised the hollow feeling it had left in her

gut. The haunting ache that she lacked something. She never wanted to be that vulnerable ever again.

He reached the door, turned the handle and looked back at her. "Do you have protection?"

He couldn't mean what she thought he did. *No way.* "Like a bodyguard?"

He grinned and Sophia wanted to wipe that grin off his pretty face with her bare hands. "No, like a contraceptive."

"That's none of your..." He moved so fast and so smoothly that Sophia blinked. The heat from his body was a tantalizing caress on her skin, beckoning her closer. She answered only to stop him from coming closer. "Yes, fine. I'm on the pill. Not that it's relevant to you."

He pushed a tendril of hair away from her temple. That stubborn lock that never stayed back. "Good." His warm breath raised the little hairs on her neck.

Knowing that he was saying it to shock her didn't stop a pulse of throbbing need between her legs. It took every ounce of her energy not to press her thighs close. She needed something distasteful, something to snap herself out of that sensual web he weaved... "You... I... You've had numerous lovers. I won't just—"

The glittering hunger in his eyes told her she'd already betrayed herself by talking as though she was considering it. *Damn!* "I'm clean."

Like a dream, feverish and hot and full of some elusive subtext, he left.

Sophia stared at the door for a long time, her knees

shaking. Covering her face with her hands, she sank back against the desk.

Luca Conti was going to marry her. Of all the men in the world, that unpredictable, recklessly indulgent playboy was giving her the chance no one else would. It was going to tangle up everything with everyone horribly. Three months of her life would change the course of the rest of her life. Even after his reckless cruelty ten years ago, she was still affected by him.

But Sophia could only obsess over one thing.

That, for three months, she could kiss him all she wanted.

CHAPTER FOUR

LUCA HAD KNOWN rejection from his mother when he'd been seven. He'd suffered debilitating headaches, insomnia and worse before he hit puberty.

The first time he'd had sex, he had been seventeen, with a woman a decade older. He hadn't really wanted the sex; he'd wanted to be held by the woman, to be less lonely for one night. Messed up as he'd been, he'd still realized what he'd done.

He'd whored himself—his looks, his charm, his body, for a bit of affection.

One didn't need a degree in psychiatry to realize that.

When Leandro had finally discovered him—his brother had always come after him no matter the time of the day, no matter how devious Luca tried to be—sitting on the floor of the hotel room with his head in his hands, and looked at him with nothing but understanding and patience and that all-consuming love that his brother used to justify arranging his siblings' lives, Luca had thrown up all over the floor. And promised himself never again.

Never again would he sink that low.

Never again would he succumb to that cavernous craving within.

Never again would he be without control.

For the most part, he was sure he'd succeeded.

Instead of fighting the sudden bouts of insomnia and crazy energy, he poured himself into everything and anything he could get his hands on. He studied like a madman, inhaling and conquering every subject he touched. He'd become a human sponge.

Leandro would sigh and smile when Luca said he wanted to try something new.

Arts and history. Mathematics and astronomy. He'd dabbled in all of them, but moved on, nothing calming the restlessness within. Only music—the relentless, endless chords churning in his head released onto paper, played until he achieved every single note—could soothe it.

It was both his release and his curse. He'd fashioned a wooden doll for Tina after she'd come to live with them, and realized he loved creating things, designing things, too. So he'd started working with Lin Huang, the creative head of Conti Luxury Goods' design department.

Through the years he'd achieved a kind of balance, a normal—for him. He wrote music for hours on end when in that grip, worked at CLG and other projects of his own, surviving on an hour or more of sleep for days. Then he had those carefree days where he got drunk, partied, took endless women to his bed. And had uproarious fun at the expense of others.

Fortunately for him, he'd discovered he liked sex,

just for itself. That he could enjoy it without whoring himself for something else. He'd slipped up only once from the happy path he was forging for himself.

Ten years ago, with Sophia. She'd been the first real thing in his life and he had let himself be carried away.

Sophia was the only one who'd ever made him forget himself, who had shredded his control so effortlessly.

For all his reputation as a self-indulgent playboy, control was tantamount to his peace of mind. It was something Leandro and he had rigorously worked on in those initial months after their mother had left. He'd spent hours on the mat mastering several martial arts disciplines.

He had an example from his father's life. He knew that like everything else he'd inherited from him, he could carry a speck of that madness—that devious, manipulative, cruel streak, too.

Control was everything to him.

Stepping out of the shower, Luca walked to the mirror and rubbed it to clear the steam. Hands on the marble sink, he stared at himself.

He looked past the compelling perfection of his features—a face he'd hated for so long—past the now bone-deep mask he showed the world. He had never lied to himself. Self-delusion would have been a welcome friend in all those miserable years.

He was doing this because of Sophia.

He was doing this because he wanted these three months with her.

He wanted to be near her, inside her. He wanted to unravel all the fiery passion she kept locked away.

He wanted to free her from the cage she put herself in; a cage, he was sure, he'd driven her into building.

But this time Sophia knew the score, knew what he was incapable of. She wasn't an innocent who mistook attraction, pure lust for anything else. This was not a marriage like his parents'.

Sophia wasn't some innocent, painfully naive young girl Antonio had handpicked like some sacrificial offering to his father's madness, to further the Conti legacy like his mother had been.

Sophia would never let herself be intimidated or drowned in Luca's personality.

The panic in him calming, Luca breathed out. Excitement filled his veins now.

For the first and only time in his life, the self-indulgent, profligate playboy he'd made himself to be was going to take what he truly wanted. And revel in it.

That he would set Sophia up for the rest of her life and do his part to protect Tina's marriage, *that* was the bonus.

Meet me @ Palazzo Reale Monday 10AM.
Don't wear black. J

The texts came on Saturday night at seven, a whole week after Luca had cornered Sophia at CLG offices. They also sent her soup down the wrong pipe at the dinner table.

Heart pounding, half choking, Sophia had escaped her family's curiosity.

She'd spent the week on tenterhooks. Wondered if she'd imagined the whole episode, if she'd somehow deluded herself into believing that the Conti Devil had proposed marriage.

When she saw Antonio come up toward Rossi's offices, she'd mumbled something to her team and skipped out like a thief.

Her reply—Why?—had gone unanswered. Which meant she'd spent half the night pacing her bedroom, and the rest of it thrashing in her bed.

Monday morning she stood on the steps of the centuries-old building, trying to ignore the curious looks from people coming and going.

She ran a nervous hand over her dress, her only nonblack slightly dressy dress. It was a sort of muddy light brown made of the softest linen. Over it, she wore a cream cashmere cardigan to ward off the slightly chilly November air.

With cap sleeves, the dress had been an impulse purchase months ago. It boasted a false buttoned-up short bodice, then flared out into a wide skirt from high above her waist.

The saleswoman had assured Sophia it made her look tall and graceful.

A quick glance in her mirror this morning told Sophia she looked neither tall nor graceful. Nothing could create the illusion when she was two inches over five.

But the thing that had made her groan was that the dress, which had fitted neatly, now sort of hung on her. Like a tent. She'd slipped her feet into five-inch purple leather Conti pumps, throwing caution to the wind.

So what if she felt like her legs would fall off later?

Whipping her unruly hair into a French plait and adding a dab of peach lip gloss, she'd been ready. Her gut twisted into a thousand knots, she had guzzled down two cups of coffee and munched her protein bar on the way over.

Minutes ticked by. Quarter past ten flew by. A couple of old men walked past her, up the steps, and she had a suspicion they were friends of Salvatore's.

Before they could catch her eye, she turned away and checked her phone. She walked up and down the steps, went back into the hall, got a bottle of water then walked back out. And all the while she waited, a sense of déjà vu came upon her.

She'd been waiting, just like this, ten years ago, too. In his bedroom, in his bed. In her underwear, albeit the sheet pulled up to her chin.

Waited for Luca, to tell him that she was in love with him.

He hadn't shown up. Marco Sorcelini had, instead, with a lascivious smirk on his face and his cell phone in hand. Before Sophia could make sense of what was happening, he'd clicked a picture of her. Told her to put her clothes on and go home…

Because Luca Conti had won the bet.

He had seduced Sophia the Shrew, made her fall in love with him and walked away. *Why else would any man touch a woman like Sophia*, Marco had added, *who was neither beautiful nor docile and far too smart for her own good?*

She'd thrown the sheet away, launched at Marco

and punched his nose. She'd lived for months in terror that that photo of her would be plastered all over everyone's cell phone. That her humiliation wouldn't be limited to Luca and his cronies.

It hadn't.

The most nightmarish day of her life and it was on repeat again. This time it was her entire family's future that she had trusted him with.

Forty minutes past ten. Frustration and fury scraped Sophia's nerves. Stupid, so stupid, to trust his word. To believe that he'd really want to help her. When everything she'd ever known of him said Luca didn't give a damn about anyone.

Just as she walked down the steps, a great beast of a bike came to a shuddering stop, right in front of her.

Black leather jacket, wraparound shades and a killer, megawatt smile that was like a shot of adrenaline straight to her heart. A small crowd of onlookers whispered behind her.

With sleek grace, Luca pulled his tall form off the bike and handed it off to a valet. Dark shadows, even worse than usual, bracketed his eyes. He looked gaunt, the curve of his mouth almost obscenely lush against the sharp angles of his face.

His jet-black hair gleamed with wetness. He looked like hell and yet, utterly, breath-stealingly gorgeous. The world wasn't a fair place.

He covered the few steps between them, looked her up and down, leisurely, thoroughly. Took the fabric of her glove between his fingers, frowned and then sighed. A twinkle shone in his eyes as it moved over her hair and her face. "That dress is not only ghastly but loose. And that color is not an improvement on black.

"You have to do better in this department if we want the world to believe we're utterly in love. I do not need extra incentive to tear your clothes off you."

Her fingers clenched tight on her phone, Sophia counted to ten. He wasn't going to reduce her to a screaming shrew in front of the whole city. "You're late. By fifty-five minutes. I…" She gritted her jaw so tight, she was going to need dental surgery. "And you look like hell. I texted you and called you, like fifteen million times. You don't reply—"

"I overslept."

"You overslept?"

"I didn't get to bed until the early morning. And I didn't want to show up here for you all dirty and un-shaved."

"You couldn't lay off partying for one night?"

"This whole thing made me nervous."

Her tirade halted on Sophia's lips. Of course he was nervous. Getting married was probably akin to being tortured for him. "Why didn't you just reply?"

"I left my phone somewhere." His long fingers were shackles on her arms. "You're shaking." He scowled. Used to that lazy, amused glance, it made him look dangerous, ferocious. "You thought I wasn't coming."

She braced herself against the concern in his tone. "I was expecting a media crew or at least those society pages social media punks to capture me standing there.

Another joke. Only this time, on a much grander scale. *Conti Devil Jilts Sophia the Stupid Idiot… Again!*"

Eyes closed, he pinched the bridge of his nose. A shadow of strain gave his usually laughing features a haunting look. "That is harsh. I never—"

"You've got to be kidding me. Was there a bet about who could seduce me ten years ago?"

"Si."

"Did you take part in it?"

"Si."

"Did you mean to disappear to Paris with your—" no, she wouldn't call some faceless, innocent girl vindictive names "—*new lover* knowing that I was—" a shudder went through her and she hated how all her strength disappeared when it came to that moment "—in your bed, naked and waiting?" Fresh out of virginity and hopelessly in love…she'd been a besotted idiot.

"Si."

"As long as we're clear, then," she added casually, when she felt like glass with tiny cracks inching around however much she put plasters over it. Somehow, she needed to channel this bitterness, this humiliation, when she was melting for one of his smiles. Because she did.

She melted. She thawed. She burned when it came to this man. She always would, apparently.

A hundred shadows drifted in his usually empty gaze. A vein beat in his temple. He opened his mouth then closed it. Wounded hesitation suited him to perfection like everything else.

Even now, she realized with a sinking awareness

of her own foolishness, she waited. As if there could be some other fantastic explanation for the cruel trick he'd played on her.

She sighed and held up her phone. "A text would have sufficed to say you'd changed your mind."

He pulled her wrist up and looked at the dial of her watch. "We're marrying in fifteen minutes."

"What?" Astonishment made her voice screechy. "I…you never told me we were marrying *today*. This morning."

"Why do you think I asked you to come?"

"To submit our documents. I brought my papers."

"All taken care of by a friend."

"The mayor's sister, I assume?"

His gaze flared and she looked away. Damn it, if she didn't keep her pride in this thing between them, she'd have nothing left. Betraying that she knew of each and every woman he'd *dated* over the last decade definitely didn't leave her much.

She turned around and looked at the building with new eyes. "Do you have any contracts for me to sign?"

"Like what?"

"Like a prenuptial, Luca." When she'd have turned, he stalled her with his hands on her shoulders. She heard him take a deep breath behind her. His exhale coated her neck. His body didn't touch her but lured her with unspoken promises.

Now his nose rubbed from her temple to her hair, his fingers leaving scorching trails wherever they touched. "What scent is that? It haunts me sometimes."

"Honeysuckle," she whispered hoarsely, even as she

warned herself this was his default. Flirting and seducing was in Luca's genes. "A small American company makes it and I buy it online." She was babbling, the only way to keep her sanity.

"It blends perfectly with your skin." His breath whispered over her cheek. "I can't wait to discover if you smell like that all over."

Liquid heat claimed Sophia, the very fabric of her dress scraping everywhere it touched. She took deep breaths, trying to not sink into his hard body.

He smelled of leather and musk, of quintessential male. Pleasure and pain, all tangled up in her head. Freedom and captivity, one inseparable from the other. He made her so aware of things she'd forced herself to ignore. Of the thump of her heart, the thrum of her skin, the sudden heaviness in her breasts, the slow, pulling pulse in her sex. Of being a woman who denied herself so many things in the name of being strong. If she'd had a boyfriend, if she'd satisfied her body's demands, maybe she wouldn't have been this vulnerable to him.

Sophia Conti, expert in self-delusion. "A pity you won't," she offered finally, a pathetic sop to a protest. She cleared her throat, as if she could chase away the desperate need. "Please tell me you talked to your lawyer."

"*Non.*"

"Christ, you can't approach this like you do everything else. You should make me sign a contract that what is yours will stay yours."

"I thought you thought me worthless."

"I'm sure just your stock in CLG is worth a lot."

Faint tension emanated from him, his roving hands clenched tight on her shoulders. "I don't care about that stock. Or the company or the legacy."

Something in his tone, a vein of disgust, alerted Sophia. It sounded so discordant, so jarring, for she'd never heard him speak in that tone before. This didn't sound like not caring. It was active loathing that hinted at a depth of feeling she didn't think him capable of.

"It's a legacy, Luca. It roots you to this place. How can you...*hate* it?"

She felt his shrug rather than saw it. "Is that why you want to head Rossi's? Don't let the idea of belonging become more important than everything else."

Faint alarm tripped along Sophia's nerves. *Was that her real intention beneath wanting to save her family? Was it an utterly selfish desire to belong?*

"Keep your hands to yourself. You're distracting me," she burst out.

The man's hands were forever roaming and roving over her. Even when she was bristling with anger. He touched as if it was as natural as breathing. Sometimes, it was affectionate, sometimes, it was provoking. But always, as if he needed the physical connection.

It was one of the things she'd loved then—being touched by him.

He laughed and continued touching her.

"This is serious, Luca. When we...separate, I don't want any accusations."

"Do you intend to take me to the cleaners, Sophia?"

"It would serve you right if I did."

"There's nothing you could do that would make me end this in a bad way, *cara mia*. Except if you fell in love with me and made a nuisance of yourself."

She laughed. A brittle, fake sound. "That is an impossibility right there."

"Then we're good, *si*? I'm aware that you're placing a huge amount of trust in me. I'm doing the same."

She had no reply to that. In her wildest nightmares, she wouldn't have imagined Luca Conti of all men coming to her rescue.

One hand landed on her shoulder. A finger stroked her nape, between her knot and the edge of her cardigan. Back and forth, up and down, until all of her being focused on that spot. "This is romantic, *si*? Us eloping like this."

She snorted. "No one who knows me would believe I'd elope."

Now the finger moved, snuck under the seam of her dress and traced her shoulder blades. "*Si*, but then I corrupted you with my kisses and my infinite charm and my dazzling good looks. I stole away every bit of your famed common sense, enthralled you. Sounds perfect when you think about it."

She flushed and looked down at herself, at the horrible dress. Would she have dressed differently if she had known? Not that she had anything in her closet that was remotely better or dressy enough for a bride.

No, this was right. Their wedding wasn't a romantic affair. It wasn't even one of those advantageous society arrangements that seemed to abound around her. It had a shelf life of three months, if that.

Her spine rigid from holding herself so tight, she blew a breath. Turned around. "Let's get married."

He smiled then, and the golden sunlight illuminated that gorgeous face. Her breath caught. He hooked his arm through hers and walked up the steps. When she wobbled, one corded arm came around her waist. She felt him look down and followed it.

When he met her gaze, there was such genuine laughter etched in his face that she smiled back. "What?"

"I'm going to take a pair of scissors and rip up all those black trousers you usually wear. You're not hiding those legs again. Not if I have anything to say about it."

They were married fifteen minutes later, in a huge cathedral-like room. Sunlight gleamed through high, soaring windows, dusting everything with a golden glow. Every time she moved, the princess-cut diamond, set in platinum, caught the rays piercing it over and over.

That he'd remembered the rings—for him and her—still shocked her.

Even the impersonal civil ceremony with no personal vows couldn't seem to dim the momentousness of the occasion.

Sophia couldn't meet Luca's eyes throughout the ceremony. Or anyone else's. Didn't want to see a mockingly wicked smile as if this was just another of his antics, another joke, just another day.

Much as she tried to not attach significance to the

day, she'd forever remember it. At least, as her only wedding day.

So the images she had of that half hour were of ancient but stylish furniture, a seventeenth-century tapestry covering one huge wall, luxurious chandeliers, brocade-covered chairs and golden-framed mirrors reflecting back Luca and her every which way she looked—she short and dowdy in her ugly dress, which she promised herself she was going to burn the moment it came off her, and Luca, looking gorgeous and a little roguish in a white shirt and black jeans that gave the best view of his tight butt.

It was a place steeped in history and for someone who'd never been able to afford sentimentality, the hall impressed Sophia. Three months later, or a year later, or even a decade later, this hall would be here, a building that had stood witness to their strange wedding.

Her wedding...to the one man she shouldn't even come near.

The clerk asked for fifteen Euros for the banns license, which Luca didn't have. "My wife is responsible for all matters financial," the rogue added with a glint in his eyes.

The wedding felt both surreal and strangely kooky. As if they were co-conspirators in a reckless game. While the truth was that she was burning all her bridges by trusting Luca.

Her family was going to be excited for all the wrong reasons. Kairos was probably never going to talk to her ever again. Society was going to laugh at her. Even she didn't believe that a man like Luca could fall in love with a woman like her. Why should they?

Suddenly, she couldn't even breathe, the enormity of what she'd done pressing upon her. She was trusting the one man who'd broken the very thing into a thousand pieces with his recklessness.

As if tuned into every doubt coursing through her, Luca wrapped an arm around her. "Trust yourself, Sophia. You made the right decision, for you."

Two of Luca's friends—a woman who worked in the Piazza del Duomo and the mayor's sister, two of his exes, *of course*—stood witness as they signed the marriage license. Neither woman, at least openly, exhibited their shock that the Conti playboy, the man who'd been called a god for his looks, was marrying the short, snarky, shrewish Sophia.

And soon, she became Sophia Conti. A solemn expression on his face, Luca pulled her close and kissed her cheek. Not her mouth, surprisingly, for a man who'd said he was eager to get her into bed.

A tender, almost affectionate caress that brought a lump to her throat.

Waving his friends off, they walked out into the sunshine. It was a gorgeous day for November.

"Let's go," he said then, pointing to his bike.

"No way am I climbing that beast in this dress."

"No way am I leaving my new bride here. Hop on, *cara mia*. I want to get to the Conti offices before they disperse for lunch. I hear they have a board meeting today."

"You want to walk in there and—" she swallowed audibly "—announce what we did?"

"You sound as if we did something naughty. And why not? I want to see the expressions on my Nonno's face. And Kairos's. And Leandro's."

Sophia wanted to see none of those people. She wanted to go home and come to terms with the emotions bursting through her before she faced anyone else. Once she processed them, she wanted to build a neat little cupboard in her mind and shove them all in there and slam the door.

"Is it necessary to upset them?"

"Stop chickening out, Sophia. You need to stop being scared of them." Which was exactly what she was doing. But for altogether different reasons.

Facing society as the Conti Devil's wife was going to be an exercise in humiliation and agony and a host of other excruciating things. But coward, she was not. With some difficulty, for she didn't want to flash him a glimpse of her underwear, she got on the bike.

With her awareness of the man and an active imagination, she didn't want to straddle anything when he was so close. The leather was supple against the tender skin of her thighs, both indecent and exciting, thanks to her libido.

"*Mio Dio!* Was that black lace and garters?" he asked the moment she settled on the scandalously wide seat.

He sounded hoarse and rough.

"You peeked? You actually peeked?" Outraged, she hit him on the shoulder, got off the bike and sputtered like a woman incapable of forming a coherent sentence. "You…you're the very devil."

He turned to the side, offering her his sharp profile. "You don't think your horribly closed-off dresses work, do you, Sophia?"

Throat dry, it took her a few seconds to speak. "What?"

"You have the lushest curves I've ever seen on a woman, *bella*. Those dresses, all they do is tempt and tease. Didn't you ever wonder why all those idiots made that bet about you ten years ago?"

All those idiots… He talked so glibly as if he hadn't been a part of it. The man seemed to have a selective memory along with a face that would tempt a saint.

And she had never been a saint.

"Because I beat them all in every test we took. Because I proved again and again that I was better than them at everything. And I didn't think they were charming princes like the rest of society did. They—" she swallowed tightly, for she'd never understood why he'd taken part in it "—wanted to see me humiliated."

That whole episode, along with being viewed as prize cattle that he could exchange for an advantageous marriage by Salvatore, everything that was tender in her, had taken a beating.

Before she'd a chance to understand her femininity, it had been crushed. So she had locked it, and any other vulnerabilities, away and continued on.

"All that is true, yes. But they were attracted to you. They thought you were the hottest girl around. They all wanted to be the ones who tamed you."

"Wild animals are tamed," she said in a tight whisper that hurt her throat.

"You can't change the world, Sophia. Men will be men—childish, arrogant and insecure. Any time we see a woman we don't understand, we call her names. All you do by hating the world is make yourself miserable."

"So I should lie down and let them beat me into what they think I should be." Because her mother, Salvatore, Antonio, Kairos, that was what they all wanted to do. They all wanted her to fit into the roles they had for her.

"No, *cara*. You fight, like you always do. You live. You count your wins. You glory in what makes you stand out and you rub their noses in it."

She smiled, finding the idea intriguing, at least in theory. "And what would these wins be?"

"Convincing the most beautiful man in Italy, *probably Europe*, to marry you, should count as a win, *si*?"

Sophia burst out laughing. He possessed an uncanny knack to make her laugh, at the world and even herself. Like a ray of sunshine in a gloomy, dank cave.

But beneath her laughter, shock persisted, an uncomfortable knot in the pit of her stomach. Every moment she spent with Luca, he tossed her assumptions of him upside down.

He saw and understood far more than the world thought he did.

Even back then, even as he'd seduced her as part of that horrible bet, not once had he tried to minimize her to exaggerate his masculinity. Not once had he called her intelligence and ambition weird. Not once had he told her to be happy with her lot.

His betrayal in the end had colored everything of that time but Sophia didn't remember a time when she'd been so easy with herself.

"You are beautiful, *cara mia*. Enough to make stupid boys do a cruel thing to get close to you."

Was that why he'd taken part in that bet, too? Hadn't he known he didn't need it? She'd been putty in his hands from the moment he'd smiled at her.

She offered a wan smile, far too rattled. "You can make the earth believe it's the sky if you put yourself up to it, Luca. I'm not falling for you."

He sighed, that dramatic, larger-than-life gesture. "Oh, you will, *cara mia*. And you'll love every minute of your descent."

Hands snug around his waist, she hung on for dear life as he took off.

In two seconds flat, wind whipped at the knot of her hair. Her dress rode up to her thighs, and her breasts were crushed against his tensile back.

But for the moment Sophia found she didn't really mind being plastered to him. In fact, she decided to enjoy it.

She decided to call being plastered to the sexiest man she'd ever meet a win.

CHAPTER FIVE

A WWF SMACKDOWN would have had less dramatic effect than when Luca, arm in arm with Sophia, rushed past an aggrieved and bamboozled set of assistants and personal secretaries, and into the conference room on the tenth floor of the Conti offices.

"I thought we should share the good news with everyone in here first."

His grandfather Antonio rose to the bait instantly. His gaze moved from Luca's face to Sophia and then to the way their bodies were flushed together at their sides. A nerve began vibrating in his temple. "What have you done now?"

"Sophia and I got married an hour ago."

"If this is one of your shameless jokes—"

Luca cut off Antonio's building tirade by throwing their license on the table.

Ten pairs of eyes went to the license, scanned it and then returned to him and Sophia.

All ten faces, two assistants and eight board members, including Antonio and Kairos, looked at him as if he had crossed that final line into insanity.

Only his brother, Leandro, didn't exhibit any signs of the panic Luca saw in the rest. But it didn't mean Luca's announcement didn't rattle Leandro. With his autocratic control of his emotions, Leandro wouldn't betray anything until he'd decided on the best course.

Luca decided it was time to make the second, thoroughly satisfactory announcement. "Since my dutiful brother has decided to abandon me and his duties toward the board, I have decided that it is time I claimed my seat on the board and directed its decisions. After all, as someone very cleverly pointed out, it is my fortune, too. And where would my lifestyle be if I didn't have the Conti legacy to live off? I have to protect my assets, push the company in the direction I want it to go." He looked pointedly at Kairos, leaving no doubt as to his intentions.

Also, thwarting all board members who'd done nothing to stop his father's escalating antics felt good. Why hadn't he thought of this before? Luca could see the fear and the shock in their faces. They were terrified that he wasn't joking, that he would repeat history. That he would be another Enzo, and that he would be left to run wild, unchecked.

Luca tapped his knuckles on the glass tabletop, letting the silence thicken with the horror of their thoughts.

Sophia next to him became stiff, as if a pole had been driven into her spine. With the pretense of pushing away at a nonexistent speck on his collar, she reached close and glared at him. "What's going on? They all—"

He stole the words from her in a quick kiss, unable to resist the temptation. He teased and taunted her honeyed mouth with soft strokes, waiting for her to let him in. She was his wife, and damn his romantic soul, he liked it.

He'd never realized what a beautiful, intimate thing that bond could be until he'd seen Leandro and Alex. That it was another thing he could never have—that connection that went beyond anything else. He'd acknowledged that a long time ago, still, his heart raced when he looked at the plain band on his finger.

Fingers on his shirt, Sophia stiffened and then slowly melted into the kiss. He licked her lower lip, an incessant clawing in his gut to own her.

She stilled, blushed and then glared at him again. Her breath was a warm caress against his lips. "You couldn't have done this anywhere else?"

He grinned. "*Non.* I want them all to see I worship at your feet."

She rolled her eyes and he tucked her close against his side.

Leandro sighed. It was that same half indulgent, half disciplinary sound his brother had made countless times when Luca had been up to something new. Leandro hated pretending about Luca. But he had proven countless times that only Luca's well-being mattered.

Amusement flickered in his brother's gaze instead of the fury Luca had expected. Luca grinned, his heart feeling light for the first time in months.

Falling in love with Alex had changed his brother.

"You barely know anything about the business or

CLG. And you hate dealing with...*people*, remember?" Next to him, Luca felt Sophia tense, her gaze swinging between him and his brother.

"I said I wanted to take an active role. Not that I would actually do any of the work."

A sort of a cross between relief and fear settled on the members' faces. One of them recovered enough to say, "What do you suggest?"

"My wife, Sophia Conti, from this day will have complete authority to make decisions on my behalf. The lawyers are preparing paperwork even as we speak. Come on, *cara mia*."

When Sophia, wooden and unmoving, only stared at him, he winked at her. Hand on the curve of her waist, he pushed her to the end of the table toward an empty chair. The members of the board watched like it was a movie.

Luca pulled the chair back, seated Sophia and then stood behind her. "Sophia has seven years of experience working at Rossi Leather. She has an MBA and specializes in risk management and forecasting business trends and marketing. For all legal purposes, she now owns fifteen percent of the Conti stock."

A ripple of shock spread across the room and for once in his life, Luca felt a sense of rightness.

He had known her area of expertise.

He hadn't told her he was giving her complete authority over his stock.

That hadn't been part of their deal. She'd never even imagined...

Eight men—the most powerful in Milanese society—looked at her as if to figure out how she had persuaded/manipulated the Conti Devil into this.

Damn it, did he really not care what happened to the company? *Or did he trust her judgment and her that much?*

That thought sent her heart thumping against her rib cage.

Sophia somehow managed to smile and nod and accept the congratulations that came her way. Kairos, without looking at her, walked out the minute the meeting was concluded.

She'd understood one thing in the show her new husband had put on.

Luca hated, *no*, despised, his grandfather. The depth of that emotion from Luca, who seemed to fairly breeze through life with no concern and with nothing but surface involvement with everyone, had rattled her.

While Luca's small exchange with Leandro had been civil, too, the bond between them was anything but. There was love between them.

After the depth of emotions she'd seen play out on his face in the conference room, Sophia wasn't sure she really knew the Conti Devil.

Her gut said one thing while her history with him, quite the opposite.

She had just started looking for him when Luca appeared in the carpeted corridor and pulled her into a small, private lounge that was the size of her bedroom at home.

Cream leather and cream walls greeted her, the

quiet luxury of the room markedly different from the business-oriented layout of the rest of the building. Afternoon light poured through the high windows, touching the space with a golden intimacy.

The most surprising thing about the room, though, was a piano that stood in the corner.

And in the middle of all that light, stood Luca, looking like a dark angel in his black jeans and white shirt with buttons undone to his chest. Dark olive skin gleamed like burnished metal, beckoning her touch. The leather jacket was gone.

The devil had intentions. And not good ones, for her mental health. Her body, however, had very different ideas for it was thrumming like an engine ready to take off.

Sophia rubbed her hands on her hips, had to swallow the butterflies in her throat before she could speak. "What is this place?"

"My brother's private lounge."

"It is soundproofed, isn't it?"

"Si." He raised a finger and shook it. "Don't ask me why."

Sophia stole a glance at the door as he closed it behind him. "You have key card access?"

"Si. Why is that so surprising?"

"I thought maybe this was the first time you came into the building."

He shook his head from side to side, making a thick lock of hair fall on his forehead. "No, I've been known to crash here, once in a while. My brother used to be a very hard taskmaster years ago. He's worked for the company since he was sixteen or seventeen. He refused to leave me alone at home."

"Where were your parents?" She'd vaguely heard of a scandal involving their father, Enzo Conti.

"Absent." The shrug that accompanied it seemed far too practiced to be real.

"So, wait, Leandro had this...room built for you?"

"Si."

She looked around the room again, noting the dark, floor-to-ceiling bookshelves. At first glance, the subjects were varied from art to space to the leather industry in Italy. "Wow, all this to just keep you out of trouble?"

"My brother takes his responsibilities very seriously."

"Why do you hate them all so much?"

A shadow flitted over his face and Sophia knew she'd hit the nail on the head. "Will you not move from the door?"

Evasion. If it didn't work, he'd smile at her. Or touch her. Or kiss her. She was beginning to see the pattern. She pushed off the door and casually strolled toward the bookshelves. None of the books were for amateur readers and looked quite worn. *Who did all these books belong to?*

"I thought it was all a joke to you. I still think a part of it is. You're like Puck in *A Midsummer Night's Dream*."

"A good-looking Puck?"

She ignored his little quip. "You do your little thing and stand back to watch the explosion. But what hap-

pened in that boardroom was more than that." She
turned around to see him standing close. Instantly,
she felt the zing in her blood. The hungry clamor
to touch him. The simple need to look at him, study
him, to her heart's content. "You let them think you
were going to join the board and for all of three minutes, that pack of gray wolves looked terrified. It was
kind of funny."

He raised a brow. "Gray wolves?"

She shrugged.

"Why gray wolves?"

"They whiff out their prey's weakness from a considerable distance. They stalk and hunt it until it gives
up out of sheer exhaustion. I have seen them all turn
on Salvatore these last few months, from the minute
things began to get worse, ready to tear *Rossi's* out and
keep the good parts. Except Leandro, and Kairos, for
his own reasons. Your grandfather leads that pack."

"So the wolves scared you, then?"

Sophia shivered. "Yes. But then I reminded myself that they need me just as much as I need them at
this point."

A sense of coiled tightness emanated from him.
And Sophia knew instinctually that he was shocked
that she'd figured him out. "Why do they need you?"

"To corral you. To keep you amused and away from
them." Her fingers shook as she rubbed her temple.
Nothing, she was beginning to realize, was simple
with Luca. And she'd hitched her already limp pony
to his ride.

He touched her then. A mere brush of his fingers

over her jaw. Sophia let the bookcase dig into her back, anything to keep her grounded in reality. "Have I ever told you how much I love that clever brain of yours, *cara mia*?"

Warmth fluttered through her stomach. "No. And you are probably the only one."

"I do." Something like pride glittered in his eyes. "And to show my appreciation for it, I'm going to kiss that lush mouth of yours."

She raised a brow. "First, tell me what that was about."

"Is it only me that finds this bossiness of yours hot?"

Another flicker of warmth. Another pocket of heat. "Luca…"

"They had the particular pleasure of seeing my father go off the rails. Now they look at me and wonder if I will do the same."

"Why you?"

"Because I'm the mirror image of him, a carbon copy. The man embezzled from his own company, used his power to prey on women and generally blazed a destructive path through every life he touched. He almost brought CLG to its knees and only then Antonio interfered. He brought Leandro into the company, and together, they ousted him in two years." There was no intonation to that statement. Yet the very bald way he said it sent a shiver through Sophia.

"What happened to him? Your father?"

"He died in jail." A vicious gleam, a dark fire in his eyes that transformed his face. To that of a disconcertingly cruel stranger. "So Antonio waits and watches, as he's been doing for years, to see if I will self-destruct like that, too. He tries to do a course adjust every few years."

Which was why he'd stalked and cornered Sophia. After Luca's latest debacle with a minister's wife, Antonio had been desperate.

But how could anyone think Luca would turn out like his father?

She couldn't imagine Luca ever preying on anyone's weakness. Couldn't imagine Luca destroying anyone's life with such malicious…

What do you call what he did to you ten years ago? the rational part of her whispered. *What he does every day with his life? How much do you really know him?*

"You—"

"I think we have had enough talk about bloodthirsty wolves."

Trying to calm her ratcheting heartbeat, Sophia focused her gaze everywhere else but him. "Why are we here?"

"To have a celebratory drink, why else?" He made a show of glancing at his watch, as if he hadn't timed all this with precision. "We have been successfully married for a whole morning."

That was when Sophia noticed the ice bucket with a champagne bottle and next to the bucket, in a cardboard box with a little bow that looked very familiar and dear to her heart, chocolate truffles.

He was seducing her; another warning from that increasingly annoying voice.

She groaned, her mouth already watering as she

imagined the dark, rich taste on her mouth. Other disturbing sensations floated beneath. She had told him once that she would sell her soul for truffles.

Countless women he'd seduced and countless little nothings they would have whispered in his ears, flushed from the good sex he gave...did he remember all those details? she wanted to ask. "Keep those away from me, Luca. They are the very devil for my diet."

His mouth pursed tight, as if he was trying to stop himself from bursting into laughter. Which in turn animated the rest of his face.

Mouthwatering chocolate, knee-melting Luca and she—locked behind a closed door.

Ignoring her plea, he tugged her toward him and raised a truffle to her mouth. "A wedding like ours, that sets at least some things to right, deserves a little celebration, *si?*"

Caught in the startlingly deep conviction in his words, his gaze intent on her mouth, Sophia licked her lips.

He groaned then, a deep, husky sound that pinged through her, leaving pockets of heat all over. "Open up, *cara mia.*"

The taste of that melting chocolate exploded on her tongue. A moan she couldn't stop escaped her throat, while his fingers lingered on her lips. Pressed at the soft cushion of her lower lip.

His gaze was hot, hungry. His mouth even hotter as he bent and swiped at her lower lip. A jolt of pleasure traveled through her, so acute that Sophia jerked.

Sinewed arms came around her, pulling her closer.

The muscles in his arms clenched under her questing fingers. Air became short in supply. And what was there was coated with the scent of him. She felt dizzy, like she was high. On him.

She licked her lips again.

He bent and dug his teeth into her lower lip. And then stroked the nip with his tongue. Liquid heat rushed between Sophia's legs. His fingers tightened over her hips. "You lick your lips like that, I will think it a call to action."

She tried to wiggle out of his hold. Only managing to press herself tighter against him. "I'm not doing it on purpose."

"I know."

His chest pushed against her breasts. Muscle and sinew, he was rock hard everywhere she touched. What the hell did the man do to have a body like that? With his lazy lifestyle, he should have had a paunch. At least a small belly. Not this washboard abdomen that she wanted to touch and lick and scrape with her teeth.

But she didn't want to let go of him. Not just yet, she promised herself. She didn't want to give up this intimacy with him. This easy familiarity that they were slipping into. The laughter they shared. The way he made her see things about herself she didn't know. She hadn't realized how deprived she'd been of this kind of companionship, how monotonous her life had become.

Maybe there were other advantages to this short marriage of theirs. The zing in her blood, the ache between her thighs, begged her to consider them. She traced the shadows under his eyes, something she'd always wanted to do. "Do you not sleep at all?"

He held her wrist and pressed his face into her hand. Leaned into her touch as if he needed it. Breath whispering like a whistle, Sophia traced the sharp angles of his face. The pad of her forefinger reached his mouth. That mouth, God, that mouth… She had such hot dreams about it.

With no warning, he turned his head, opened his mouth and closed it over her finger. And then sucked it. A hungry, stringent pulse began at her sex, in tune with the pulls of his mouth.

Her skin felt too tight to hold her. The silk of her panties was wet. Rubbed against her inner thighs as she shifted restlessly.

He released her finger. Sophia clenched her thighs closed instinctually, needing friction there.

A dark flush dusted his cheekbones. He knew, oh, God, he knew. He knew where she was burning to be touched.

"I'm an insomniac."

It took her several long seconds to realize he was answering her question.

He was an insomniac? "How bad is it?"

"I sleep a few hours every few days."

"That's it? I need at least eight hours every day to feel remotely human. Doesn't that have side effects?"

"It does. But I have learned to live with them."

It made him more three dimensional, more… human. As strange as that sounded. "What do you do, then? In all that time?"

Fingers busily shifted the collar of her dress. His mouth landed on the skin he bared. His tongue licked that juncture, sending hot shafts of pleasure down her spine. "Do you taste like silk all over, Sophia?"

"Yes," she said, completely lost in the magic he wove. She tried to recall some warning, some common sense as to why she shouldn't be in his arms, pressed up snugly against him. With him sucking on random parts of her.

Zilch. Nada. Nothing came up.

Then the diamond on her ring finger glinted, a twinkling ray of common sense. She ordered her body to stiffen, to move away, but it had different ideas. "We can't be doing this. We can't… If you gave me that power over your stock thinking that will make me grateful, thinking I'll happily—"

"Spread your legs and take me inside you?" He was the one who pulled back. "You really think I'd have to pay for sex? I'm not sure who it reflects badly on that you think that, you or me. Or have you truly become as cynical as they call you?"

He castigated her so softly and yet Sophia felt his words like tiny pricks. "Then why?"

In response, he dipped his mouth and took hers again. This kiss was not an invitation or a tease. It was full-on assault, demanding surrender. Almost brutally efficient in the way he slowly but surely made her into a mass of shuddering sensation.

She'd made him angry, Sophia realized beneath the avalanche of sensations. His tongue laved the interior of her mouth, while his hands moved up and down her body, inciting her into a frenzy.

Expert strokes, here and there, perfect pressure, a master of seduction at work. A routine.

His heart wasn't in it. He was seducing her with technique and experience. He was proving a point. She could be a tall, blonde model for all that it mattered to him.

The difference, even as heat drenched her, sent bile up her throat.

"No, Luca, please." She sank her hands into his hair and tugged his face down. "That was moronic. What I said," she finally whispered, her hands molding and tracing the line of his shoulders. "I…have never been able to believe that someone like you could want someone like me."

She didn't want to mention the bet again. It was in the past. But she saw his understanding of it, saw those same shutters come down.

He sighed and instantly gentled. A devil so easily calmed with honesty? A man whose feelings could hurt under that almost impenetrable mask he wore? She wasn't so sure anymore that she knew him.

Across her temple, then over her nose, and then her jaw, he placed soft kisses. "I kiss you because you're thoroughly kissable, Sophia. I kiss you because I can't bear the thought of those lush lips not quivering under mine, of that stout will not surrendering to me. I kiss you because I want to hear that sigh you release when you realize this fire between us is too hot to fight. I kiss you for that moment when your shoulders lose that stiff line, when you melt into willing softness. I kiss you for that moment when you make that little growly sound in the back of your throat, as though you've just realized that you've been a passive spectator. I kiss you because then you take over the kiss, you forget why you should resist me and you devour me as if I was your favorite dessert in the world."

He whispered the last words against her mouth. As if he was infusing her very blood with those tender words.

She sighed.

Then she groaned.

Then she kissed him back with a ravenous hunger. All things he'd predicted. He knew her so well, even in this… It was a faint warning at the back of her mind that dissolved under the influx of such delirious pleasure.

His lush mouth delivered on the fantasies it promised. Hard and soft, sometimes masculine demand, sometimes a tender entreaty.

Vining her arms around his nape, she stretched to reach more of him. He was right; she hated being a spectator. One hard thigh pushed in between her legs, but didn't quite hit the spot.

When she shifted, one hand landed on her thigh, pushed up her dress and then pulled her leg up and around his buttocks.

His thigh moved even farther between her legs. And up. Right against the hungry core of her.

Shamelessly, Sophia clenched her thighs and then moved on his leg, back and forth. Up and down. Plea-

sure spiraled through her pelvis, building to an unbearable rhythm.

Teeth banged, tongues sucked. Clasping his jaw
with her hands, she held him for her delectation. Then
she dug her teeth into that carnal lower lip, hard, and
sucked it into her mouth.

A growl rumbled from his chest. A wild beat
danced in her blood as she realized something had
changed between them. Tension radiated from his lean
frame. His fingers became more urgent, his mouth
harder and hotter.

Playtime was over.

His fingers crawled into her hair, tugged at the clip
she'd used to pull it back into a tight knot. The clatter
of the clip against the wall where he threw it was a
bang in the hoarse silence. Fingers pulled and plumped
her hair until it fell in unruly waves around her face.

She forgot what she'd meant to ask him. She forgot
what had disconcerted her so much about the scene
in the conference room. She forgot why she shouldn't
kiss him like this. Only sensation mattered. Only the
heat building inside her mattered.

He moved his thigh away and she whimpered. She'd
melt into a puddle if he didn't hold her up. Her mouth
was stinging, her blood singing; Sophia was so aroused
she was ready to beg him to finish it.

He lifted her leg again, pushing away at the ugly
dress. Up and up. Until the lace of her garters was visible and then a strip of her thighs. "Sophia." He was
panting against her cheek. "This is where you put a

stop to it if you don't want to be bent over that table and have me thrusting inside you in three seconds."

Reality came crashing with that crudely worded statement. He'd put it like that on purpose. She growled, a demand and a plea twisted in that animal sound. He laughed, took her mouth with his again.

She jerked away from him, stumbled on jelly-like legs and then reached for him again to steady herself. "No," she said, running a hand over her mouth.

All she wanted was to cry. Her mind felt soaked in desire, frustration. "God, I came looking for you because I wanted to talk." His pupils were dilated, his chest still falling and rising. But he didn't look the least bit put out for being denied the same satisfaction. "I didn't mean to hump you like a dog in heat. You're not angry?"

"I'm in considerable pain, yes..." He sighed "I'm not angry. I know you'd like to believe the worst about me but I do have a little self-control."

"Oh, is there anything I can do to—"

"You can fix your dress and stop offering to help. Next time you offer, I'll ask you to go down on your knees."

O went her mouth again. An instant image fluttered through her brain. Did he ask it of all his lovers? Did they do it because they didn't want to lose his interest?

Personally, Sophia had always thought the act a little subjugating, undignified and maybe even a little painful to the participating woman's mouth. "Do you ask it of all your lovers or—"

"Stop talking, Sophia," he growled again.

Sophia dashed into the attached bathroom. She splashed water over her heated cheeks. His fingers had built her hair into a cloud around her face. She looked soft and feminine and like a woman who lost her mind after two kisses.

Damn it, she had the most important meeting of her life in a few minutes and here she was, climbing all over Luca. He was like her craving for that chocolate truffle. A bad habit she thought she'd beat only to succumb again and again.

He'd suggested she fall. And she was falling gloriously. She thought herself above all those women who threw themselves at him. How bitchily righteous she'd been... If anything, she was even more foolish because she'd already had a taste of him ten years ago.

She'd thought herself beautiful, special to have attracted his attention. And it had been nothing but a bet. "Maybe deprivation will build a little character," she said, coming out of the bathroom.

Could she sound any more naively hopeful, any more sanctimoniously righteous? She couldn't, *absolutely* couldn't care if he satisfied himself with another woman that night.

He was scowling. "We're both consenting adults and have been joined in the holiest of bonds in front of God and man just this morning. You're making us both walk back out like horny dogs. You have enough character, don't you think?"

He sounded so pained, so disgruntled, that Sophia burst out laughing.

It was easy, far too easy, to be mesmerized by Luca's

easy charm. As long as she remembered that there was nothing of substance beneath. "I scheduled a meeting with you and Leandro in an hour."

"Your plans for Rossi Leather are ready for Leandro?"

She nodded, barely bracing herself against the admiration in his eyes. "I want to run them by you and Leandro first before I present them to Salvatore. That way, we're all in the loop."

How was it that with of all the men she'd dealt with—CEOs and ruthless businessmen and millionaires—it was this wastrel playboy that was never intimidated by her? Who only showed respect for her accomplishments and her ambition.

Could that easy confidence come from just his looks? Or was there more to Luca than met the eye?

He uncorked the champagne bottle and poured it into two flutes. Handing her one, he clinked his against hers. The bubbles kissed her throat on the way down. She looked up to find his gaze on her. Rattled by the line of her thoughts, she said nothing.

They talked of a varied range of topics, sometimes agreeing and more than once, getting into a heated argument. Only when her watch pinged did Sophia realize how invigorating and informative their discussion had been.

And how enjoyable.

Throughout the meeting with Leandro and Luca, all Sophia could think of was how jarringly discordant, how disconcertingly different this side of Luca was from the man she'd despised for so long.

CHAPTER SIX

THE LAST THING Sophia wanted, after the events of the last week, was a party.

A party thrown specially in honor of Luca and her.

A party to which every member of the high society of Milan was invited, including men who'd known of her humiliation ten years ago.

A party thrown by her in-laws, the Conti family, which was a minefield of dysfunction—her family seemed so normal even with her differences with Salvatore—she couldn't imagine navigating without setting off an explosion.

The last she'd seen of Luca had been outside the Conti building, six days ago. He'd called a taxi for her after her meeting with Leandro and him and then driven off. The invite for the party came later that night, in the form of a phone call from Leandro's wife, Alexis, her new sister-in-law.

When she'd moaned about attending, Salvatore had warned her that she couldn't alienate her husband's family. *Her new family*, in fact.

To which, she had, quite forcefully and uncharacteristically, asked him if he was that happy to be rid of her. Only silence had remained then. Full of guilt and shame, Sophia had apologized to him and left.

She'd never confronted Salvatore like that. There had never been any need. Since he had married her mother, he'd been kindness itself to her. He'd paid for her to go to University, given her a job at Rossi Leather, provided her with everything she could have ever asked for.

The only thing he didn't give her was his trust when it came to business matters. Could she blame him when it was a one-hundred-and-sixty-year-old legacy that he wanted to protect for her brothers? Maybe asking for him to take such a big risk on her, when she'd never really excelled at the things he wanted of her, was too much?

Maybe things would have been different if she'd been born a Rossi.

At least, she had done the right thing in marrying Luca. Salvatore was delighted that finally he had a connection to the venerable Contis.

Sophia had come to Villa de Conti straight from work that evening, and had been shown into Luca's suite by a smiling Alexis. Aware that she'd wanted to chat, Sophia had claimed a headache and rushed in for a bath.

After her shower, Sophia put on a silk wrapper and stepped out into the bedroom. Her impulse purchases lay in chic, expensive bags on the bed, having left a hole the size of a crater in her bank account. Designer heels lay in another box.

The glittering bags mocked her. She flopped to the bed, feeling foolish now for splurging—when the devil hadn't even answered her texts. *Again.* Was he going to show up tonight?

She'd just rubbed lotion in and put her underwear on when the door opened quite rudely. Cursing, Sophia grabbed her towel just as Valentina, of all people, came into view.

Spine rigid, Sophia preempted the tall beauty, who looked stunning in a long black evening dress. "I'm far too nervous already, so please, Valentina, no theatrics right now."

The younger woman had the grace to look ashamed. "I came to apologize, Sophia." When Sophia remained stubbornly silent, Valentina changed tack. "My brother sent me to see if you wanted help."

"Thank Leandro, but I'm good."

"*Non*, Luca sent me."

The towel slipped from Sophia's hands. "Luca is here? Downstairs?" Her breath ballooned up in her chest.

"*Si.*"

He hadn't deserted her. Just for this evening, Sophia needed him by her side. After tonight, after getting through facing the society that she'd never belonged in, she wouldn't need him again.

"You thought he would not come?"

Curiosity filled Valentina's question. The last thing Sophia wanted was the Contis or anyone else for that matter, to know how little familiarity she had with Luca's lifestyle. "I'm nervous because I know everyone's eyes will be on me and I don't handle attention well."

Valentina's gaze swept over her almost clinically, assessing, and Sophia tugged the towel toward her. "You are hot, Sophia, why do you hide it?"

The question was so matter of fact that Sophia forgot that she was supposed to be angry with Valentina. "Did he ask you to be kind to me?"

"*Non*, I'm not being kind. He did tell me to stop being bitchy to you." The woman didn't mince her words and Sophia was beginning to like her. "You have breasts I would kill for." To punctuate it, she looked pointedly at Sophia's breasts, contained dangerously in a pink bra and then at her own relatively smaller ones, which wasn't saying much because everyone had smaller breasts than Sophia's.

And then Valentina sighed.

Sophia half groaned, half choked.

"I developed very late and even then, they were like apples. Yours are more like…" Sophia wanted to crawl under the bed sheets. "Small melons."

"Please, Tina…stop!" Sophia rubbed her fingers over her forehead, shook her head and then let the laugh building in her chest escape. Tears filled her eyes, her nose, she was sure, was running and her throat and lungs burned. "Oh, how we torture ourselves… I've always been so jealous of your model-like figure, your style and grace. You're like a gazelle, whereas I…waddle like a penguin. Your sense of fashion is…just wow."

Warmth entered Valentina's eyes, transforming her entire visage. "Sense of style and fashion can be…

acquired, *si*? But not curves. Unless I go for those silicone implants. But I don't think Kairos will like artificial boobs and there is already too much he…" Stricken black eyes shied away from Sophia's. "I know now that Kairos and you are just friends."

"You confronted Kairos?"

"*Si*. He was angry that I struck you. *But*… I had no business acting like a bitch to you. Not when the problem is between us." Misery radiated from her. "Will you forgive me, Sophia?"

Sophia smiled. "If you help me, yes. Since you're a fashionista who Milan looks up to, can you advise me? I bought three dresses. I don't want them to see a wobbly penguin paired with a strutting peacock. I want to look back on tonight and not cringe." There were far too many cringe-worthy episodes already in her life.

Valentina burst out laughing. "My brother is a peacock?"

Sophia nodded. With a brisk efficiency, Valentina vetoed all three dresses in two minutes flat.

"The saleswoman assured me that they are the height of—"

"*Si*, but she followed your direction to cover up every inch of skin. What is in the last bag?"

"That one… I picked that one. But it's going straight back to the shop. I don't know what I was thinking."

Valentina floated through the room, picked up the last bag on the bed. The knee-length turquoise silk slithered out in a silken whisper. "This dress is perfect."

Alarm rattled through Sophia. "That was a foolish

purchase. It is strapless and too snug and my *melons* will surely pop out and then—"

"What are you so scared of, Sophia? That people will realize you're beautiful under the hideous clothes you wear?"

"Hey! They're not hideous and—"

"Fine, look like a penguin, then. There will be at least three women downstairs who have, at some time, been linked with Luca."

Sophia gasped. "Oh…you play dirty."

No way was she going to be shown up by Luca's willowy exes. Tonight might be a farce, but *she* was going to be the heroine of the farce.

A thousand butterflies flying in her stomach, she let Tina do her hair, even her makeup. When Tina pronounced her ready, she faced the floor-length mirror. Her breath halted in her throat.

The low cut of the bodice showed the upper curves of her breasts. Simple beadwork on the bodice caught the light with every breath she took. The hem of the dress kissed her knees just so, baring her legs. She turned her foot and looked at her legs. She did have sexy legs.

The woman in her, the part she tried to hide and ignore and forget, preened that she looked good in it. Nothing was going to make her tall, elegant or graceful but that was okay. She would continue her diets, grumble about never being svelte but she would also enjoy what she was. No more hiding, as if she was ashamed of herself.

Rub their noses in it…

Her hair, air dried during her chat with Tina, fell in dark waves, softening the strong planes of her face.

Bright red lipstick, brighter than Tina's, made her mouth look scandalously seductive. Like her red lips could somehow balance the rest of her features that she'd told herself were far too stubborn for a woman. "This is too red. It will make everyone look at my mouth—"

"You married the Conti Devil. Of course they will look at you. Why not give them something gorgeous?" She looked Sophia up and down with a strange glitter. "How like my artistic brother to see what you so carefully hide, to see what no one else could."

A cold shiver snaked up Sophia's spine. "Luca is artistic?"

It was Tina's turn to look surprised. "Luca is a lot of things that I can't even keep track of. He works for CLG only to please Leandro. He has a personal…" She threw Sophia a startled glance. "Leandro even calls him our very own mad genius. Apparently, Luca's musical talents have no comparison."

"In a fond, useless sort of way, right?" Sophia asked, her heart thundering in her ears. "He lives off his brother and his family's fortune and dabbles in music, surrounds himself in beautiful things, that kind of artist?"

Her nose high up in the air, Valentina flayed her with her gaze. "That indulgent playboy thing he does— that's only one side of him. Your marriage to Luca, I know that it's an agreement for a few months. That he lets you use him in them. But still you should know that—"

"I'm not using him as much as we're using each other," Sophia interrupted, in prickly defense. Of course, the devil would try to come off as her savior in his account of their deal.

"Luca is not all he seems, Sophia."

Luca works at CLG, just to please Leandro.

Luca is artistic.

Luca was turning out to be more complex than any man she knew.

Sophia halted on the top of the stairs, trying to corral the panic spearing her belly. She tried to let very little in life unsettle her—in that way, she and Luca were alike, although with him, she supposed it was easier, more his natural state.

At least, that's what she'd assumed.

Even taking a couple of deep breaths didn't calm the furor in her veins. She couldn't get a grip on why it mattered this much.

All she knew was that she needed him to be what she and the entire world though him to be. A wastrel, a playboy. A man who cared for nothing and no one.

She appeared at the top of the curving marble staircase like a beautiful thought from his mind come to life. Luca felt a pressure on his chest, as if there was weight there, making it harder to pull a breath. He'd known, and guessed, she would be a revelation.

Oh, but what a revelation she was…

He heard the stunned whispers behind him, like a gathering wave rushing toward the shore.

The gasps, the *bellissimas*, the frantic reassessment of a woman they had all been duped into not seeing. Joy sang through his veins. The same he felt when he finished a piece of music or when he manipulated stock numbers into a pattern, into making sense. Like seeing a piece of art, unfinished and raw, come to life.

His joy in her was possessive and primitive. Suddenly, he didn't want anyone else to see her like this. He didn't want the whole world to see and covet this beautiful creature.

She was his, at least for now. He wasn't arrogant enough to think he'd created her but he'd discovered her, hadn't he? He alone had seen what Sophia was beneath that prickly nature and tough attitude. And tonight, she was a true reflection of the woman beneath—soft and yet formidably beautiful.

He wanted to pick her up, throw her over his shoulder, carry her away to his studio and lock the world away. He wanted to bury himself deep in her, until neither of them could breathe, until he was rid of this obsession with her. Until her mind, body and spirit, they were all only his.

He'd never chased a woman before. They all came to him. That he was chasing a woman who was determined to not be caught by him was perfect irony.

The bold, sensual lines of her body were a feast. The upper curves of her breasts swelled over the strapless bodice, beckoning to be savored. The silk followed the dip of her waist and the flare of her hips, lovingly touching everything he wanted to.

Their eyes met and the world floated away.

Her brown gaze raked over his face, lingering, assessing, almost frantic in its search. A clamor began in his veins as he stood at the foot of the steps and she took each step down.

Shards of light from the crystal chandelier caught at the white beads on her dress. And glinting brown eyes. They didn't look average or dull right then.

They glinted with a fierce intention.

She looked at him as if…she wanted to peel off all the layers he covered himself in and reach inside the core of him. A shiver traveled down his spine.

As though she'd somehow bypassed the surface sheen of him—his looks, his charm. As though she hungered to know more.

But he couldn't reveal himself to her. He couldn't show the dirty truth of his birth, couldn't show her the devouring hunger for something more than he was allowed to have. Only then would this work. And he was so lust-riddled for her that Luca would have taken even a morsel of Sophia.

By the time she reached the last step, he'd calmed himself down. His practiced smile curved his mouth.

She raised a well-defined brow, all haughty arrogance.

He imagined that was how she commanded her team at work. One raised brow and one blistering remark from Sophia would probably send the staunchest soul scrambling to do her bidding. She wielded it with the same skill now, he thought, as if to start the evening with swords drawn.

All it made him want to do was kiss that brow. And probably her temple. Then that stubborn bridge of her nose. That lush, carnal mouth. Then he would bite, none too gently, on that defiant chin.

A line of fire swept along his nerves at the delicious path he could trace down her glorious skin. Very soon, he promised himself. Very soon he'd have her all rumpled and flushed beneath him, screaming his name. Only he would unravel all that strength she wore like armor. Only he would know the soft, vulnerable woman beneath.

He could have had her that day at the CLG offices but he didn't want to see her regrets later. He wanted Sophia present and pleasantly ravished when he was through with her. "You look biteable, *cara mia*."

She looked startled at the compliment, looked away then back at him. Had he done this to her? Luca wondered for the millionth time. Had he shattered her confidence so badly?

"Nothing to say, Sophia?" he prompted softly.

"You disappeared for six days, three hours after we were married." Accusation punctured every word. "Even for the short-term agreement that our marriage is—" She bent toward him, her voice lowered to a husky whisper, for she was flushed with awareness. "You can't just rush me into a taxi and walk away. I ate a ton of chocolate and probably gained three pounds in three days. Do you know how many questions I've faced just from my family alone? Salvatore is desperate for your plans for Rossi's."

"But they are your plans."

"Yes, but he doesn't know that." She slowed down her words as if he was a bit slow in the head. Luca had never had so much fun just talking to a woman. "I told him Leandro and you are finalizing them. Damn it, Luca, there has to be some accountability even in this sham. We didn't even talk about where we'd live."

Her whisper caressed his jaw; the honeysuckle scent of her wafted over his nostrils, tightening every muscle and sinew. Acres of glowing skin taunted him. He shrugged, struggling to get a grip on the desire riding him. Hard. "I've never been a husband before, so you have to forgive me. I will check in with you every night at eight. *Si?*"

She sighed, and that made her glorious breasts rise and fall. "Wonderful. Now I feel like your parole officer."

"Will you put me in handcuffs if I violate my conditions, then?" he offered and saw her swallow visibly. "I could not give up control like that for any other woman, *bella.*"

Desire shone in her enlarged pupils, a song sung by her hurried breaths. She licked her lower lip, took it in between her teeth, flushed and then pursed it into a thin line. As if she could hide her mouth.

Three hundred people waited for them and he was painfully hard.

Dio, when had lust ever taken control of him like this? Six days and nights he'd spent cooped up in his studio, and he'd still not gotten it under control.

He didn't like needing her so much. He didn't trust himself in this state for he'd never been in such before. He intended to ravish her out of her senses, not lose his own.

"If anyone asks," she said, coming to stand by him, "and by that I mean my mother, we aren't doing a honeymoon because I'm super busy. And you, too."

A tiny sneer curled her mouth every time she talked about his "work." Or lack of it, to be precise. It made him want to pull that snobby upper lip into his mouth and suck on it. He would do it, too.

He was going to need a little notepad to jot down all the numerous things he wanted to do to her. Suddenly, three months felt like a very short time in which to indulge his darkest fantasies with her, to drive her from his blood, once and for all. Especially because the woman was an obvious workaholic.

Urgency laced with his desire now and he ran a brave finger down her jaw. She swatted him away, like he was a fly. "You want her to believe this is a love match."

"Of course I do."

He nodded. "It'll probably break her heart to see her daughter doesn't have a romantic bone in her body."

She rolled her eyes. "Her daughter can't afford a romantic bone. Anyway, we steal all kinds of time during the day to see each other and get up to all kinds of..."

He raised his brows and waggled them. Warmth tinted her cheeks, the brown of her eyes gleaming bronze. Oh, she wanted him, all right.

"Afternoon sex—how delightfully imaginative, Sophia."

"I had to say something when she burst into my bedroom and demanded to know why I wasn't with my beloved husband on my wedding night."

"Why do you live with your parents? Doesn't that curb your nightly…activities?"

"I don't have any nightly…" She clamped her mouth tight, her face flushed. "I…work a lot of late nights and I like to keep track of what's going on with Sal and the company… It's just easier that way."

Again, a pang stole through Luca. Had he so thoroughly crushed her heart that she had no romantic notions left like any other woman?

"I do regret not spending our wedding night with you. Did you wait for me to spirit you away?"

She flushed and it lit a fire inside him. "You're absolutely cuckoo. I can't stay with my parents anymore. Not if I want to have some peace to work in the evenings."

"So move into Villa de Conti. Into my room. Alex and Leandro don't stay here all the time. Neither will I distract you, except when I feel like it. But—"

She hissed. The woman hissed at him. "Where were you? And why do you never answer a single call or a text?"

Luca raised a brow. No one ever asked him where

he went and when he came back. Not even Leandro, after he had reassured himself that Luca wasn't going to self-destruct. The novelty of it was amusing and a little disconcerting.

"Here and there," he said, tucking her arm through his. "I can take society only in small doses." Which was more truth than he'd ever confided in anyone. "After the drama in the conference room that day, I needed time to recoup."

"Time to recoup?" she repeated, but with more consideration and less belligerent disbelief this time. Like she was thinking far too much again.

Dio, the woman really needed less thinking, worrying and planning and more ravishing in her life. A good thing he was so committed to it.

"*Si*. But now I'm ready to be your adoring husband." He smiled then and brought her to the huge ballroom.

He frowned as the music filtered through him.

A string quartet was playing. There was dynamics, articulation, wonderful fluctuation to the tempo but no soul to the music, no risk-taking except perfectly executed sharps and flats.

The lifelessness of it jarred through his head. A near compulsion ran in his veins to either yell for the music to stop or to stalk out of the room.

"Luca?" Sophia prompted.

Neither option was feasible, though.

Pasting on his megawatt smile—the one that had once driven a tempestuous young woman to avow love

to him in the midst of her own engagement party—
Luca turned to her. "Yes, *bella mia*?"

Light brown eyes studied him like he was a fly
under a microscope.

Not the effect he intended in that perceptive face.
Not even that endearing snort or roll of her eyes. "The
music, you don't like it?"

Pure panic bolted through Luca for a second. As
if every facade he had built over the years was being
ripped away, leaving him utterly stripped of his armor.
To face who he was, what he was capable of, in front
of the whole world and see the horror he'd seen in his
mother's eyes. He couldn't bear that look in Sophia's
eyes. "Do you know what is happening with Kairos
and Tina?"

"No," she said with an arched look that told him
she saw through the ploy. It was becoming harder to
pretend with her. Like his mask was slowly but surely
cracking, giving her glimpses of him. "We spoke
briefly, though."

She offered that tidbit reluctantly as if Kairos
needed her protection. From Luca. She gave so much
of herself to just a friend. "What did your friend say?"
he asked casually, swallowing away the jealousy her
friendship with another man aroused.

"That he'll be waiting to offer his support as a
friend *when you leave me in pieces*, to quote him. I
think Tina is causing major ripples in his life."

The goodwill he heard in her tone for his sister
warmed Luca's heart. It confirmed his growing belief

that Sophia had only ever wanted Kairos's friendship. "Why do you assume that?"

"Because he said 'We should have never gone near those *Contis*' in a pained voice before he hung up."

Luca laughed. "Good for Tina," he whispered in Sophia's ear and pulled her onto the dance floor.

CHAPTER SEVEN

TONIGHT, SOPHIA DECIDED, as she tried to not search the huge ballroom for Luca like a desperate, clingy wife, she could be a deer. Never a gazelle or a swan, but at least not a penguin—and unlike the last Conti party she attended, this time she was not a skunk.

She also, quite uncharacteristically, decided to put away all the things Valentina had said about Luca into her newly commissioned cupboard in her head. Tonight she wouldn't worry, plan, obsess, hide or hate. Tonight she would take a leaf out of her playboy husband's colorful book and enjoy herself. She'd dance, drink and flirt with Luca, even. Maybe.

It was without doubt the best evening of Sophia's life. Suddenly, it seemed, all of society, the same people that had always looked on her with begrudgingly given kindness wanted to talk to her, invited her to posh luncheons and generally wanted to figure out how she'd corralled the Conti Devil.

Even knowing that Luca had been with half the women there, Sophia met a few women whom she'd love to get to know more. It was as if by lowering her own walls, she could see the others clearer, too.

And with a haunting clarity, she realized how right Luca was. She'd always been different in this strata of society, which in turn had made her defensive. Thirteen, unpolished but streetwise, she hadn't trusted that Salvatore wouldn't change his mind about keeping her; she'd decided from the first moment that she didn't belong there. Instead of risking rejection, she'd built a wall between her true self and everyone else. And then that episode of the bet had given her even more reason to hate them all. A shield, she realized now.

She danced with Luca, who was, of course, a graceful, slick dancer, then with Leandro, who to her surprise, told her she was welcome to come to him for any matter regarding the CLG board. Almost as if he'd been warned by his brother to not offend her.

Kairos was away on a business trip, thankfully.

Then there was Antonio, whom she'd avoided all evening. Sheer cowardice? Yes, but Sophia didn't want him to ruin her perfect evening.

Luca heard the snick of the door behind him and sighed. He'd come into Leandro's study, looking for the legal papers he'd asked Leandro's lawyer to draw up.

Without turning, he knew who it was. He'd been waiting for this confrontation all week. Dreading it. Loathing it.

For his grandfather was quite adept at turning Luca back into that needy, emotional boy he'd been during those hard years. Unable to manage his headaches and his restlessness, unable to sleep.

Cowardly as it had been, hiding out in his studio for a week had an added advantage to it. Antonio never ventured there. For one thing, Leandro had decreed long ago that it was Luca's space—sacred and safe and inviolate. For another, the studio was evidence that Luca had inherited more than just his father's good looks.

Antonio preferred to believe the Contis were invulnerable to anything from simple mood swings to brilliance-induced madness. Even after Enzo's life proved otherwise.

"You cannot give Sophia power over CLG stock or your seat on the board."

"I already have," Luca retorted. So there was at least no pretension to niceties to be had. He grinned; riling up Antonio was a task he'd enjoyed immensely even as an innocent child. "You have hounded us for years to marry. You even picked her as the perfect Conti bride. For the first time in my life, I agree with you. Sophia is perfection."

"You do this now only to mess with all of us."

Trust Antonio to know Luca as well as he did. "Sophia is my wife and has my best interests at heart."

Antonio scowled.

The thought that riled Antonio more than Sophia sitting on the board was a bastard, self-made man like Kairos taking his place at the head.

"Let her be your proxy. That controlling stock of Contis should lie within the family members."

Luca shook his head. "This fixation you have about the glorious Contis needs to be contained, *Nonno*. Haven't you done enough damage in the name of it?"

His grandfather flinched, backed a step as if Luca would attack him physically. Provoked as he'd been, Luca had never done that.

"All I ever did was to make sure your father didn't ruin our family name."

His head jerking up, Luca watched, stunned. Antonio had never offered a defense before. "You knew your son better than anyone. You hushed up so many little things he'd been doing all his life. You should have seen what he was becoming. You should have protected her..." He turned away, breathing roughly, mustering his emotions under control.

"You accept Sophia or you don't." He shrugged. "I've no problem cutting you out of my life, unlike your dutiful grandson Leandro. But she will continue on the Conti board even if I have to legally give her all my stock."

Rage filled Antonio's eyes. "She...married you because I suggested it."

"What the hell are you talking about?"

"Your affairs, your reckless disregard for our name... I was desperate. So I went to her. I thought she was the one woman who could handle you. I offered her a fortune if she brought you to the altar."

Luca smiled easily, more amused than affronted by Antonio's revelation.

Sophia had never hidden the fact that she'd do anything for her family. *Dio*, he knew with a faintly increasing alarm that half his attraction to her was based on that. It was her beauty, inside and out, that enthralled him.

He wanted Sophia untouched by the dirt in his family, away from the unrelenting grasp for power, the manipulations.

He wanted her to be only his, in his moments of light, separate from the dark, self-loathing part of him. But he'd not only brought her into it, he'd made her two powerful enemies already—Kairos and Antonio.

"You give her even a single share of Conti stock and I assure you, you will never see any of it back ever again. She might not be Salvatore's blood but she is as grasping as he is."

Luca couldn't care less, if he tried, about what Sophia would take from him. "Go to hell, *Nonno*. And say hi to your son while you're there."

"I did not offer her up, your mother, like a sacrificial lamb to him, knowing what he was." Luca stopped at the door, knuckles tightening on the knob. Antonio, for the first time in his life, sounded old. Frail. "He married her in secret, just like you did Sophia. He could be even more charming than you, when it pleased him. He claimed he was in love and I allowed it. I thought she would bring balance to his life…calm him. He was happy enough for a while. Your mother… *She married him*, Luca, of her own free will."

It had just struck eleven when Sophia realized she hadn't seen Luca's prowling gait in the ballroom for over an hour. The party was in full swing, champagne was flowing, couples still dancing.

Now she wondered if he'd disappeared. Again.

Apparently, Luca was like a mirage, present for as long as it took to entice and lure. Only to disappear the second you got close.

She had drunk three glasses of champagne with Valentina and her friends. Imagining the calories in three drinks, she'd delicately munched on glazed carrots and fruit from the scrumptious buffet.

The result was that she was mildly buzzed. She walked the perimeter of the huge ballroom, smiling and nodding at people she didn't even know. A woman pointed through the corridor with a perfectly manicured finger and a malicious smile.

Sophia's buzz evaporated as if someone had siphoned off the alcohol from her brain. Strains of husky laughter, of the female variety, greeted her from one open door. Luca's deep tones followed the husky laughter.

Ice slithered through her veins, rooting her there.

Run, run, run. Her brain issued flight responses as if the threat was fatal.

One breath and then another, Sophia forced herself to concentrate on just that. No, it was only her pride that chafed, she reminded herself. It was only sheer disbelief at the man's utter lack of decency. Her heart was stout and uninvolved.

They had no claim on each other, true. He hadn't promised her fidelity, this time or the last. But he wasn't going to show her up as a fool again.

One evening, *Dear Lord*, one evening was all he'd given her and already…he was smarting at the reins? She hadn't even demanded much of him.

She marched into the room, somehow managing to not fall on her face in four-inch heels.

The room was another lounge offering a view of Lake Como. It seemed there was an endless quantity of those at Villa de Conti but not enough distance from his family for Luca. Another fact she'd gleaned tonight. He'd happily offered her a place here because he never was here.

Was there anyone or anything Luca didn't need escape from?

A piano was the focal point of the room and on the bench, with his fingers desultorily playing with the ivory keys, was Luca. A stylish, contemporary chandelier threw patches of light onto his sharp profile.

The notes, though played slowly and haltingly, made up a haunting tune that plucked at Sophia's nerves. At some heretofore unknown place that had become arid from neglect.

A stick-thin blonde sat on his left on the bench, her silk-clad thigh flush against his, leaning over him to reach the keys. Which, from Sophia's angle, clearly showed her lemon-sized boobs—*thank you, Valentina, for that*—rubbing against his upper arm.

Luca stilled, all sleek and wiry strength, but Sophia didn't wait to see if it was in anticipation or in defense. *She'd had enough!*

Refusing to give in to the urge to run and grab the blonde by her hair, which would give credence to her reputation as a shrew, she walked, sedately, toward the couple so seemingly immersed in each other that they didn't notice her.

"Please take your paws off my husband," she said with a sweet smile that hurt her cheeks. "Also, get out of our house."

The blonde had the grace to look ashamed at being caught out. Sophia fisted her hands, fighting the urge for violence. If *lemon-boobs* so much as smiled at Luca, she was going to lose it.

But the woman, perhaps sensing that Sophia meant business, stood up, slid out with a sort of gliding grace—*another damn swan*—and left the room.

Sophia counted to ten, went to the door, closed it and then leaned against it. Wrenching herself under control. Seeing the stick-thin woman sidling up to Luca… It ripped away her own self-delusions. Her pathetic reassurances.

God, when had she begun lying to herself?

When had she started believing that she was the Sophia that the world saw? How had she believed she could resist this man?

How had she convinced herself that she could take him on and come out unscathed at the end of these three months?

After his talk with Antonio—somehow, his grandfather managed to sink under Luca's skin every time, like an eternal monument to the darker aspect of his life—Luca had felt an overwhelming need to disappear. Antonio had known what his revelation, about Enzo falling in love with his mother, would do to Luca.

Caustic fear had beat a tattoo in his head that he was like Enzo in this, too, that he was beginning to buy into his own pretense that all he wanted was fun with Sophia.

Had his father married his mother with the best intentions? Had he meant to keep his promise to love her and cherish her? Had he thought he was in control just as Luca thought he was with Sophia?

Had he been aware that he'd become a monster toward the woman he'd loved and yet hadn't been able to stop?

Rattled by Antonio's revelation, he hadn't gone back into the ballroom. To her.

He had not followed the blonde, nor touched her. But he'd been sorely tempted. Here was the way to delineate from the path his father had taken, the only way, it seemed, to retain control of this farce that was already pulling him under…so destructively simple— to touch the nameless woman, to sink into her inviting body and prove to himself that his defenses were intact.

That he was intact.

Only he had looked at the woman and bile had risen in his throat.

Would the ghost of his father haunt him here, too? Was it not enough he'd passed Luca his looks and his madness? Would he now drive him into humiliating Sophia?

Even for a farce, she would never forgive him. And that was one thing Luca couldn't bear.

He faced himself every night in the mirror and only self-loathing remained. He was never alone in his head; he was never alone when he looked in the mirror.

So he'd stopped looking and lived as best as he could. But if Sophia looked at him like that...*non!*

So he stayed. A little weak. A little undone. And a little ragged in his hunger for her. He wanted to be inside her. He wanted to learn everything there was to know about her. In that wanting, Luca realized there was no one else.

No one drove his actions, not stupid bets from which he thought he would protect her; no one whispered in his ears that this, too, was already set. Nothing but pure, scorching desire motivated him. No ghosts of mad fathers or distraught mothers. Nothing but Luca and his desire for her.

He was alone in wanting Sophia, like he wasn't in anything else.

She stood there, plastered against the door. Stubborn chin tilted high in challenge. Luscious breasts fell and rose as she battered at her temper, beating it into submission.

She would not win tonight, not against him, not against her own nature. She was his. The only question was how much she would make him chase her.

But it made sense, that she was different in this, too. That she demanded to be chased, demanded to be won over.

He wanted nothing less for his wife, anyway. Half turned away from piano, he raised a brow. "That was quite impressive. Alex would have nothing on you if you decide to be mistress of the manor, or the estate in this case."

He wasn't grinning, which was strange in itself. She'd have thought he'd love seeing her struggle with her temper. Second, there was an almost somber quality to his expression.

"You couldn't contain yourself for one evening?"

"So the claws are out?"

"Claws are all I have." Damn it, how could she be feeling this sense of betrayal? Had she not truly changed where it mattered?

No, she had. She'd grown a shell to keep the world out while hiding away herself. Even convinced herself that she didn't need or want anything or anyone.

Until this moment.

And she was truly seeing him this time, now that her own naïveté was gone. Now that she didn't have to hide from herself. "No pretty feathers like your... *numerous friends*. Did you—"

"I have quite the craving for claws, *cara mia*, when they are yours. So stop threatening and start using them."

It was said in a voice taut with challenge. Not mocking or teasing. Shadows moved in his eyes where there had been nothing but insouciance before.

Sophia felt like she'd locked herself in with a predator. Gone was the easy, charming Luca that she could handle, if not admire. This man who looked at her with darkly hungry eyes was not he. He seemed edgier, less controlled. More real.

Back down, a voice whispered. *Back down and walk away.*

Sophia smothered that voice and shoved it out of her head. No force on earth could make her leave the room now. Not now, when maybe, there was a chance she could understand why she was so drawn to him. Why this…madness claimed her so easily when it was Luca Conti.

"I'm a novelty to you right now. But you can't help it, can you?" She couldn't let him bespell her with such words. "You attract women like you were honey and they bees. It's probably coded into your DNA—"

"She. Followed. Me." His nostrils flared. A pulse flickered in his sculpted jaw. Dark fire leaped in his eyes, a lethal warning. "It's a little disconcerting how much the idea of a quick screw with another faceless woman holds no appeal right now."

A sense of coiled danger radiated from him and the woman in her, instead of being terrified, wanted to court that danger. Wanted to sink under his skin and burrow there. Wanted to leave a mark on him this time, like he'd done on her.

Like a moth called toward a column of fire, she went to him. She straddled the bench, uncaring that it pulled the dress to her thighs. That it signaled so many things that she hadn't even realized she was ready for.

The air around them thickened. The party outside melted away. Slowly he moved closer. The masculine scent of him filled her lungs.

"You didn't discourage her. You didn't push her away. You sat there and let her paw you. You didn't act like a man who wants another."

Something gleamed in his eyes, a sudden, violent energy radiating from his frame. His hands curled around her nape and pressed none too gently. The rough scrape of his fingers against her tender skin zinged through her entire body like an electric charge. He dipped his head, and licked the rim of her ear. Arching her back, Sophia closed her eyes.

Deft fingers pulled away her chandelier earrings. Teeth nipped at her earlobe. A surge of liquid desire went straight to the place between her thighs.

Lights and stars behind her eyelids.

The soft tinkle of the earrings as they hit the marble floor threw her a rope toward sanity.

The devil was distracting her and how well. For now, his tongue was licking inside her ear. "You want a claim on me yet you refuse to even wade in?"

"If you're going to make a fool of me again, look into my eyes and admit it."

Her scalp tingled as long fingers sank into her hair and tugged hard. Exposing the curve of her throat to his mouth. Hot and open, he breathed the words against her skin. "You'll not make me feel guilty for something I haven't done."

His fingers were over her bare shoulders now. Stroking back and forth, up and down, reaching lower and lower over her neckline. Her nipples puckered when he almost touched one on the downward trajectory.

He didn't.

She gritted her jaw hard to keep from crying out. From begging. She was sure that was what he wanted of her. Utter surrender. "Then why can't you just say 'I wasn't going to touch her'?"

She was desperate for him to say he had no intention. But he didn't. Because Luca never lied. The thought of his mouth on that blonde let out a feral anger in Sophia.

"Why set the rules for a game you're too cowardly to play?"

"It's not enough they chase you day in, day out? You can't let one go even when you're not interested?" His hands stilled.

Why couldn't he, for one evening, be hers and hers alone? "Is your self-worth that low? Is it their adulation you crave?"

His arms returned to his sides, abandoning her aroused flesh. He stood up from the bench and walked away. Panic bloomed in her stomach. "I think I've had enough of this drama, this marriage business, for one day."

Denigration, disinterest; it was a slap to her face. Carefully orchestrated to hurt her, to push her away.

There had been such amusement in his eyes that day at the board meeting. But underneath it, Sophia had also felt something else. And when she'd asked him about it, he'd distracted her.

It had definitely short-circuited her brain and stopped her from pestering him. But she now saw it all clearly. Like an expert writer, he'd controlled the narrative at the board meeting—from their open shock and fear that he might start taking part in the Conti board politics, to suspense for his own shockingly deep reasons, and then, finally, to relief that it would be Sophia who would take his place.

Presented without that convoluted act, they wouldn't have tolerated her presence in their midst, much less welcomed her opinion. But by presenting her as an alternative to him and the mischief he could wreak, he'd forced them to accept her.

Luca was not without control.

Luca was control. He walked it like a tightrope. Every breath, every smile, every word, every gesture, it was all done with a purpose.

"You control what everyone thinks about you." *But why?*

CHAPTER EIGHT

HE GROWLED FROM across the room. This horrible noise that came from his throat, as if he were a ferocious but wounded animal and she the hunter.

She got off the bench and moved toward him.

"Your affairs are always splashed about. There's always some drama at some big party where you behave abominably. The only time one of your affairs wasn't splashed about was with me."

Now his hands were fisted by his sides.

Somehow, that disgusting bet had never reached anyone's ears. Of course, she saw the knowledge of it in those friends of his over the years, taunting and offensive, but no one had actually dared say a word about it to her face. Or spread it around that the chubby geek, Sophia Rossi, had fallen for the devilish Luca Conti.

"Will you give me sainthood now for *not* making a public spectacle of you, Sophia? Are you that desperate to justify this?" The sneer in his voice struck her like a stinging slap.

She bucked against his tone. But she didn't break

and run away as he intended. She reached for him and leaned her forehead against his back.

Warmth from his skin radiated through his shirt. Hands shaking, she pulled his shirt out of his trousers. She sank them under it, frantic in her search for bare skin.

Skin like hot velvet, the muscles bunching under her touch. She moved her questing hands around to his abdomen. Up and down, like he'd done with her. Ropes of lean muscles. And his heart thundering like a ram under her palm.

He was a study in stillness, in tension, in rejection. Every inch of him was locked tight. Another push and he would lash back at her, would break her.

But how could she back down now?

She'd always thought of his looks as the gateway to his arrogance, to his indulgent lifestyle, but now she wondered if they weren't just a mask, hiding so much more than they revealed. Every woman was blinded by his smile; every man wanted to have that natural, effortless charm he possessed; everyone willingly bought into the role he played.

She'd bought it, too, all these years. "You…you perform, Luca. For Antonio, for Leandro, for Tina, for the entire world. You have created this specter of you and you use it to keep everyone at a distance."

He turned and Sophia braced herself for his attack. She was learning him now, learning when there was a hint of the real Luca and when it was the abhorred playboy.

Something changed in his face, then. An infinitesimal tightening of those razor-sharp cheekbones. A thinning of those lush lips. A glitter in those eyes that were always quick with a smile and a comeback, usually laden with sexual innuendo.

He seemed to see straight through to the heart of her—the fears and desires, everything she kept locked away to get through hard life. "You want to have sex with me. Desperately. You crave it and yet, you can't give in to the inevitable. So you look for some redeeming quality in me.

"I shall never be the man for you, Sophia. So, if you are not going to screw me, at least stop pretending."

She blinked, dazed by how much he saw. How accurate he was.

Both of them were right. Both of them saw far too much of the other that no one else saw. And both of them were far too gone to back out now.

He was hers in that moment, Sophia knew. Against his own better judgment perhaps. And the fighter in her reveled in this victory, in wrenching a part of him away that no other possessed.

He could have been with a million women but it didn't matter. Not anymore. She had a piece of him no one else had.

She vined her arms around his waist. Tension thrummed in every line and sinew of his body. His fingers gripped her wrists tight enough to leave marks, intent on pushing her away. And she was the one who calmed now; she was the stronger one in this moment.

"What do you want, Sophia?"

She let her body slowly mold itself against his. "I want you to make love to me, Luca."

His thigh shoved in between her legs, his hands on her hips, pulling her tight and flush against him. He was long and hard and unbearably good against her throbbing sex. The jolt of heat that went through her was instantaneous, all-consuming.

Their eyes met and held. No challenges were issued. No deals were made. There was nothing but will and heat and the desire to burn together.

The neckline of her dress was tugged and pulled, her nipples left knotted and needy. Fingers busied themselves with the zipper at her side now. Breath was fire in her throat. Fever in her blood. The ripping sound of the zipper scraped against her nerves. Cool air touched her breasts and she gasped. Still no fingers where she needed them.

"Interesting." Hoarse voice. Clipped words through a gritted jaw. Muscles under her fingers clenched. Lean body pressing against her suddenly became tense. "No bra."

"Backless dress." Cool as a cucumber she sounded, while she was incinerating on the inside. A breeze touched her skin and she shivered.

"You are like hot silk. I'm going to lick every inch of you."

She closed her eyes and heard him shed his shirt.

Long fingers on her back—gentle, kneading, almost possessive as they pressed her toward him.

Breasts flattened against skin, hot and velvet-soft stretched taut over tight muscles. Nipples rasped.

Hands in her hair held her like that, their torsos flushed tight against each other. His shaft lengthened and hardened against her belly. Her sex clenched and released, hungry for his hard weight. Their breaths rattled in the silence. He took her mouth then.

Soft and slow, his kisses were like honey spreading through her limbs. Roaming hands touched her everywhere, restless and urgent, belying his tender kisses. "Sophia?"

"Hmmm?"

"I should very much like to be inside you now, *cara mia.*"

Only now did she focus again on the people a little distance away. Music and laughter. She stilled at the prospect, her pulse in her throat. "Here? Now? They are all…right there."

Fingers tightened in her hair. "Now, Sophia."

It was his way or not. He did this to her on purpose. Pushed her into this corner where she realized how desperately she wanted him. Pushed her past her own boundaries into new territory. Like she had done with him.

He expected her to back off. He expected her to shrivel and hide and ask for the cloak of a bedroom and the dark night.

"Yes," she whispered, pressing little kisses to his chest. Flicking her tongue out, she licked the flat nipple and tugged it between her teeth. She pressed a trail upward to his throat and then closed her lips over his skin. "Here, now."

She felt the shudder in him then. And it was another small victory.

When he turned her, she went. Her will was not her own now. Her body was his to do with as he wanted. "Look at us, *bella mia*," he whispered at her ear.

Sophia looked. They stood in front of a gilt-framed mirror, below which stood an antique writing desk. Two chandeliers cast enough light to illuminate every inch of the huge room.

Light and dark, soft and hard, he lean and wiry and she…voluptuous and flushed, they were different in every way. Skin pulled taut against those sharp features, he was a study in male need.

But she was…she was the one who looked utterly erotic.

No rouge could make her cheeks that pink. Her pupils were large, almost black. Her mouth was swollen, unashamedly wide and seductive. The pulse at her neck throbbed as if someone had pulled at it like a string.

The turquoise silk hung around her hips, baring her breasts. Her nipples were plump, distended and meeting his gaze in the mirror, Sophia felt like she was scorched to the very core of her.

"What do you see, Sophia?"

She closed her eyes, her breath coming in short puffs. "I look indecent. Like everything I want is written all over my face."

"I see a woman whose curves and valleys are as complex as her mind. I see a warrior, a seductress, and I see a woman who hides her heart from even herself."

His words were just as powerful as his caresses. His fingers moved restlessly over her flesh, stopping here and there, pressing and kneading, but never staying. Learning and pressing all over—the rim of her ear, the line of her spine, the demarcation from her waist to her flaring hips, the crease of her thigh, the fold of her elbow…

There were so many other places crying for touch but he didn't touch her there. Her dress slithered to the ground and she stood in just her wispy lace panties. Then those were pushed down, too.

Sophia barely processed it when he turned her and then lifted her onto the table, as easily as if she were a china doll. The wood surface was cold against her bare buttocks as was the wall at her back. Yet, she was burning up all over.

Eyes wide, she watched as he kicked off his leather shoes and socks and then those trousers and black boxer shorts.

He hardly gave her a breath to savor the tall, darkly gorgeous form of his before he stood between her legs. Rock-hard thighs pushed her own wide, baring the heart of her to his wicked gaze. He took her hand in his, kissed the underside of her wrist and he pushed her palm against the heat of her.

Sophia jerked at her own touch.

"Are you wet for me, Sophia?"

Brown eyes widened into molten pools in her face, she looked so innocent.

So pure. So hot. So perfect.

The equation between them was changing and morphing, and all because he had oh so cleverly thought he could control himself. So full of himself, he'd forgotten Sophia was an explosive variable... Joke was on him. Rarely had anyone ever surprised him like Sophia did.

She saw far too much. She didn't tread lightly even in this; she marched in, banners raised, breaking walls down, determined to reach the part he hid from everyone.

It should have sent him running. Instead, here he was.

He was alone, always, where it mattered. It was the only way he could live. But that she saw him, even such a small part, in this moment, he didn't feel alone.

He felt a connection. He felt like someone knew the true him. He was weak enough to want to hold on to that for a little longer. Human enough to want to protect this. Just a little longer, he promised himself. No lasting damage this time, he'd make sure. Only pleasure for him and her.

"What?" she said, all spikes and thorns.

"Take your lovely fingers and dip them into your—"

She kissed him then and swallowed his filthily provocative words. Hard and fast, desperate and a little fierce, until he was deluged in sensation. "If my fingers would do just as well as yours, I wouldn't be here, now, would I?"

Acres of glowing skin, pouty, lush breasts, plump nipples begging to be sucked into his mouth, soft belly and a cloud of brown curls hiding the velvet heat of her.

Wide eyes sparkling with desire and curiosity and possession. Such an irresistible combination of strength and vulnerability. So strict even with herself.

She was the most real thing Luca had ever seen.

His lovely Sophia. His lioness, his warrior, *simply his* in this moment.

He wanted to stay in that moment forever. But it could not last. Whatever it was that tugged at them relentlessly could not last. Because he was Luca Conti.

So he did what he did best. He reduced this moment of excruciating intimacy to nothing but animalistic sex. Into nothing but raw heat and primal possession.

"Is it not enough that I'm here, now, Luca?" she finally murmured. Her breath was stuttering. The pulse at her neck throbbed.

"No, I want more, I want everything, Sophia," he whispered, and felt her name move through him like a powerful invocation. "Tell me, did you touch yourself the night of our wedding?"

"Yes," she answered tightly.

"Did you finish?"

"No. It wasn't… I've never before…"

He bent and pressed his mouth to the upper curve of one breast. Her nipple rasped against his chest, taunting him. He gripped the table until his knuckles turned white, his erection pulling up tight against his abdomen.

But there was a keening pleasure in the need riding him hard.

Every inch of him felt alive. Every inch of him felt like a pulse. Denial, even for a few moments, was an alien concept for him. He had so very little, so he reveled in what he could have. He glutted himself on it.

Sexual gratification, once he'd stopped whoring it out for other things he'd needed desperately, was the most uncomplicated thing in his life. But now anticipation was like a drug, heightening every sense, a fever in his blood.

He opened his mouth and sucked on the tender skin. Hard. She was salt and desire and delicious on his tongue.

Nails digging into his shoulders, she convulsed against him. Not pulling away but pushing into his touch. So he did it harder. Her moan reverberated around them. "Touch yourself and tell me if you're already swollen. Take the edge off."

"No." Defiant chin lifted. Demand sparkled in her eyes. And a challenge. His erection lay stretched up against his belly now, engorged and ready. She moved her hands down the slopes of his shoulders to his chest. A pink nail scraped against his nipple. A finger traced the line between his pectorals.

He waited on a knife's edge, his breath bellowing through his throat.

Featherlight and fluttery, her touch made him ache. Everywhere in his body. He felt like that cavernous hungry thing that was his mind had taken over his body now. All he was was desire. As if answering his unspoken request, she touched his painfully thick erection.

No tentativeness, no hesitation, as she wrapped her fingers around the hard length and pumped him, up and down. He thrust into the circle of her elegant fingers and growled. Covered her fingers with his own and showed her how to do it.

"I'm a very fast learner," the sexy minx whispered as she stroked him just the way he liked it. Hands on the wall on either side of her, head bowed down, Luca closed his eyes and let the pleasure wash over him.

Honeysuckle and something of Sophia filled every breath of his. "In your mouth now, Sophia," he demanded roughly.

She would back off now. She hated being told what to do, didn't she? She hated anything that she thought made her weaker or exposed or vulnerable. And of all the people in the world, she'd never bow or bend to his commands—

He tensed as he felt the tentative slide of her tongue over the head.

Dio in cielo, she looked up at him, a wicked smile in her eyes and then her wide mouth closed over the tip of his shaft. His head went back; his vision blurred as he slid into the warm crevice of her mouth.

"Like that?" she whispered when she slid him out, her pink mouth wet, her nudity a luscious invitation.

Challenge and entreaty. Siren and slave. Desire and defiance. He had never seen a sight, heard a sound, more beautiful than her. For the first time in his life, he had no saucy retort, no way to reduce this into simple carnality. How when only Sophia and her wicked mouth would do?

She flicked her silky tongue over the slit and repeated her question. He saw stars, and sky and pleasure so blinding that he couldn't breathe. His hands sank into her hair, holding her in place. He had meant to disarm her; he had meant to somehow bring the chains of this thing between them back into his control.

Instead, he felt unmanned. Distilled to his essence, stripped of his armor.

Sweat dampened his skin as she continued her little ministrations with an eagerness and efficiency that pushed him closer to the edge. There was a fever in his muscles and he found it was he that was shaking now. Coming inside her mouth would be heaven but more than that, he wanted to be inside her, he wanted to see her face when he finished, he needed to drive her to this same…bewildered, out-of-control state she drove him to. He needed to be one with the incredible woman that was cajoling, stealing, wrenching away parts of him.

He pulled her up in a hurry of need, never having felt this sense of urgency, this potent urge to feel and revel. Pressed his mouth to one softly rounded shoulder before thrusting his thigh between hers. Against his muscular, hair-roughened thigh, she was like satin silk, a sweet haven.

"Luca?" she whispered, her eyes impossibly round in her face. The innocent but curious interest in it pounded in his veins.

Dio, was there nothing about the woman he could hold against her? Even in this, she shed her inhibitions, willing to go wherever he took her.

He delved his fingers into her folds to test her

readiness. Pink spilled into her cheeks, a spectrum of browns in her eyes. She was slickly wet against his fingers. He stroked the swollen bud there and she jerked into his touch, demanding more. Twisting her chin, he kissed her plump mouth. "First, I need you like this, *cara mia*," he offered, before he took himself in hand and pushed into her wet sheath from behind.

The tight fit of her flesh stroked every nerve in him, a flare of heat pooling at his groin.

Her gasp, throaty and husky, tore at his nerves. Desire and lust, need and something more, everything roped together, all independent flames merging together and setting him on fire.

He met Sophia's eyes in the mirror and Luca believed everything in his life—every ugly thing he'd lived through—was all worth it, if it had brought him to this woman in this moment.

Sophia scrambled to keep a millionth of the wits she possessed, for she didn't want to miss a single moment of being possessed by Luca. She wanted every sense open, for she felt like she was turned inside out, every secret, every fantasy, exposed. In this position, she didn't know where she ended and where he began.

He had made it good ten years ago; even her virginal body huddled under the covers on his bed, had known it. Even as she had refused to let him turn the lights on, look at her in daylight. He'd handled her with tender caresses, reverent touches. However ugly his motives, he'd made seeking and giving pleasure a beautiful celebration, made her body feel like an instrument of pleasure instead of a source of shame.

But this was different. She was not an awkward girl who didn't know what to do with her suddenly voluptuous curves or the sudden, unwelcome, indecent attention from the same boys who despised her guts. She was not ashamed or confused by the demands or the reactions of her body.

Now she was Sophia Conti, the devil's wife, and it had already changed her. For better or worse, she had no idea but it was irrevocable. She owned him in this moment and she owned her sexuality.

Instead of distaste, as her expectations had been about this experience, she felt like she was an extension of him. Or he of her. Instead of shying away, she boldly raised her gaze and met his in the mirror.

Smoothly contoured shoulders framed her slender ones. Dark olive skin, stretched tightly over sinew provided an enticing contrast against her skin. Nostrils flaring, plump mouth pursed in passion, he was magnificent. And so was she, the perfect female counterpart to his masculinity.

Dark fingers moved from her hips, across her rib cage to cup and lift her breasts. He rubbed the turgid peak lightly, then moved to the other one. But even the gossamer touch was too much when she held his hard heat inside her. She clenched her inner muscles, the need primal, instinctual.

He pressed his forehead against her shoulder, a guttural growl coming from the depths of him. He didn't withdraw, but rotated his hips and again, Sophia clenched around him.

Sensation spiraled, inch by inch, until Sophia felt even the jerk of his hot breath against her skin like a stinging caress. They stayed like that, learning each other and testing all the different ways they could move against and with each other, their bodies in perfect harmony, the tension building to an unbearable pitch.

Sophia was afraid she would fragment into a million little pieces if she didn't climax soon. She held on to his forearms and pressed herself against his chest. "Luca?"

He licked the pulse beating frantically at her neck and spoke against her skin. *"Si, cara mia?"*

She arched her spine and pushed back into him, until he was more deeply embedded within her. Voluptuous pleasure suffused her at the hard length lodged inside her. Head over her shoulder, she looked back at him, half-delirious with need. "I'm dying here, Luca."

A quick stroke of his fingers at her clit made her groan wildly. "All you have to do is ask, *bella.*"

She panted, struggling to form a thought. "Please, Luca…don't make me wait anymore. I need you. I need this like I've needed nothing in my life before."

Long fingers gripping her hips with such deliciously tight pressure, he pulled out of her. All the way before thrusting back into her again.

Sophia arched her back, threw her head against his chest.

Her breath came in soft little pants, her channel

still trying to accommodate his large size. Every inch of her sex quivered at his stark possession. At the unbelievable pleasure pulsing up her spine. Her thighs shook under her, her knuckles white where she gripped the table.

There was no technique, no experienced caresses. This was raw, real. And so damn good that she thought she'd implode from the inside.

A palm on her lower back pushed her down and she bent, malleable and willing. Like heated clay in his hands, his to do with as he wished. Another hand quested toward her breast, plumping and molding.

Her entire body was like a bow for him. Long fingers pulled expertly at her nipple before moving down, down to tug at the sensitive, swollen bud at her sex again.

He thrust in again, his fingers and his hard length applying counterpoint pressure over her throbbing flesh to his rough, upward thrusts. Pleasure screwed through her pelvis again, nearly cleaving her in half. Sophia sobbed, screamed.

"*Dio*, Sophia," he whispered, before withdrawing and pushing in again.

The intimate slap of their flesh, the slick slide of their sweat-dampened skin, there was nothing civilized or romantic about what he did to her. He was not the experienced lover whose technique and skill in lovemaking was rhapsodized about in silkily whispered innuendoes. He was not the masterful seducer.

With her he was desperate, his thrusts erratic, raw, his need nothing orchestrated. With her, he was just a man who was as desperate for her as she was for him. He took her, savage and uncompromisingly male, and Sophia reveled in it as she climaxed in a wild explosion of pleasure. Fingers roughly holding her down, Luca thrust in a long stroke and then he was convulsing against her, a rapid stream of filthy Italian words filling her ears.

Sophia smiled and decided they were the sweetest words she'd ever heard.

CHAPTER NINE

"MALEDIZIONE, SOPHIA! Stay away from Antonio."

Sophia stilled as Luca, for the first time since she'd known him, raised his voice. He stormed into her brand-new but mostly bare office on the floor newly given over to displaced Rossi staff in the CLG offices in the heart of Milan's business district.

"I have kept every promise I made. What more could you want from that manipulative old bastard?"

Her newly appointed assistant, Margie—Sophia had never had an assistant or an office or even a stapler of her own before—stood staring at Luca, her mouth open wide enough to catch any stray butterflies. The woman had to be fifty and yet, like clockwork, a faint gleam of interest appeared in her eyes and she abruptly straightened out her shoulders, sucked her tummy in and thrust out her meager breasts clad in a thick wool sweater.

Bemused, Sophia turned to Luca. Who was completely unaware of anyone but her in the room. Like nothing but Sophia in the entire world had any consequence to him whatsoever. Whether meetings or parties, whether they were surrounded by a hundred guests curious about their marriage, or just at an intimate dinner with the Rossis—they hadn't socialized much with his family after the party, as if he wanted to keep her separate from them—Luca had the addictive habit of zeroing all his focus on her.

A woman couldn't be blamed for getting used to being looked at like that. For misunderstanding fiery lust for intimacy, camaraderie for affection. For starting to believe in her own fairy tale that she could tie the charming, incredibly insatiable Luca Conti to herself.

Thick hair disheveled, sporting a stubbly beard along with the constant blue shadows, and dressed in a rumpled white Polo T-shirt and blue jeans, her husband looked like a thwarted grizzly bear. An utterly sexy and thoroughly disreputable version.

Her husband; she was calling him that far too frequently, even if in her head. She was becoming possessive, and she had no idea how to stop.

She sighed, waiting for the stinging awareness that took over her body every time he was near to lapse into a bearable pulse.

Luca, she'd come to learn in four weeks of their all-too-real-feeling marriage, was given to bouts of intense restlessness, which usually signaled that he was going to retreat, from which he emerged a day or two later and then followed furious social activity.

The restlessness wasn't violent or physical as she had learned the night she had found him sitting at the veranda, staring into the pitch-black of the night. It was in his eyes, in the detached, distant way he looked at everything around him, in the long walks he took around the estate as if his energy was boundless. In the warning that radiated from him to be left alone when he was in such a state.

But when he emerged from it, it was as if he hadn't been absent for hours.

She'd hurried back from work one afternoon to Villa de Conti, intensely relieved to see his bike and marched straight into the shower. A wicked glint in his eyes as he watched her, water caressing his hard body. "Please tell me, *bella*, that you came home for an afternoon quickie."

"This is not funny," she'd said then, fighting off his nimble fingers. He'd still somehow shed her of her linen jacket, leaving her in her stretchy camisole.

"Luca, this is serious."

His knuckles traced her nipples, tight and wet against the fabric. "I have a new appreciation for your starchy suits, *cara*. I feel like a kid unwrapping a present every single time I undress you. Only I know the treasure that is beneath."

"We can get help." Her hair plastered to her scalp and her mascara ran down her cheeks. For once, Sophia didn't give a damn how she looked. "I did some research and there are all kinds of new research to beat a drug addiction." It was the only thing that made sense.

To which he had replied that he didn't do drugs, kissed her and then proceeded to show her how *she* could calm him down. He had taken her then, against the wall, under the onslaught of water, with swift, desperate, hard thrusts, his mouth buried in her neck while she had halfheartedly and nearing climax, objected that this was the opposite of calming.

She had no idea what calmed that restless look in his eyes or why he needed to escape.

For a lazy playboy, the patterns of his days and nights were utterly demonic. Her mind reeled at the highs and the lows, at the chaotic clamor that seemed to be his life. She couldn't imagine surviving the erratic quality of his days and nights, the lack of structure… How could he get anything done?

He doesn't do anything, remember? a voice whispered. The shrew, as she had taken to calling that voice, the one she'd developed to distance herself from anything she sensed might make her weak.

But he hadn't once left her hanging.

He'd given her every bit of his attention in numerous meetings she'd had with Leandro and him to reinvent the Rossi brand as a subsidiary of CLG. First she had had to sell Leandro that Rossi was still a household name, prove that it had upped manufacturing standards in the last five years, a project she'd overseen personally. Then she'd shown him sales numbers proving that when it came to belts, men's wallets and other niche leather goods, Rossi was still beating CLG.

"And here I thought you were taking my brother on a ride," Leandro had said drily, pinning her with his implacable gaze.

Once Leandro had come on board, she had taken on Salvatore.

Which had needed a show of support from the Conti brothers—even Sophia had been impressed by the complementary strengths of the brothers, one silent but reeking of power and the other charming but persuasive. An agreement that CLG signed saying it would never do away with the Rossi name *and* endless business proposals, finally convinced Salvatore.

Though he'd grumbled when she'd suggested discontinuing any Rossi products that competed directly against CLG and instead develop a range of more complementary products. Luca had managed to convince Sal in a matter of minutes that Rossi's had sunk because it could never compete with CLG and yet kept trying to, a point she'd been trying to make for several years now.

An official press release said CLG was investing in Rossi's to make their renowned clutches, belts and other accessories, redesigned to meet the luxury standards of CLG and enter the market again.

Sophia had been appointed as the director of overseeing the first production line from design to marketing. An appointment that hadn't filled Sal with confidence until Luca had winked at him and said, "Good to keep someone from your side in there, Salvatore. You can't trust my brother or Antonio completely."

When she'd thanked him with a kiss on his cheek, he'd grinned wickedly. "I love this whole man behind the woman concept with you, *bella*. Although I like being above and under you, too."

Leandro had watched them with something like shock in those gray eyes.

She'd hidden her face in his chest, her throat dangerously close to tears, and pretended to find his lascivious comment obnoxious. He'd warded off the emotional moment with humor. As always. But Sophia didn't believe that Luca was shallow anymore.

The truth was that he was weaving himself into every part of her life, into her very being. All too frequently now, Sophia wondered what she would do when he was gone from her life.

Who would she cry to about Salvatore? About the entire species of men? Who would make her laugh? Who would drive her to the edge of ecstasy? Who would hold her in bed as if she were the most precious thing in the world?

She ran a hand over her stomach, as if she could calm the panic. "Hello, Luca. Do you like my new office?"

He pushed a hand through his hair and walked around, his long, sinuous body overpowering the space immediately. Then he turned to her with a frown. "You should have one with a nicer view. Not the one looking at the back alley."

Smarting at his dismissal, Sophia said, "I don't care about the office so much, Luca. Salvatore has agreed to let me pitch the idea for—"

"You should care, Sophia. As long as you act like you deserve only this much, that's all you get. All these years, you have let Salvatore box you into a position that you were overqualified for. You—"

"I was learning the business, every part of it."

"What is your excuse now? Why are you still pussy-footing around him?"

"Too many things have changed in the past few months. He needs—"

"He needs to hear you say that this is your company as much as it is his. That you're the best thing that's happened to it in the last decade. Have you decided to neatly play in the boundaries you set for yourself, afraid that if you push, he might tell you you're not his daughter after all? Have you decided that is all you could have, Sophia?"

It felt like the ground was melting away from under her feet. Like something she hadn't even seen was ripped open for everyone to see.

Like she was standing naked in the midst of a crowd, her worst nightmare, all her toughness, her strength, her pride, mere illusions. She was that little girl again, desperately pretending that she was not scared at the prospect of leaving the only home she knew. Her throat felt raw. "You don't know what you're talking about."

He reached her then and the tenderness with which he clasped her jaw was enough to break her. She should hate him, this man who saw past everything, but she couldn't. "What will you do when I'm done with you? How will you convince Sal of anything then?"

All Sophia heard in that little outburst was *when I'm done with you*. Her entire world felt colorless, lifeless, in that sentence. "I haven't thought that far ahead."

"Then you aren't much of a planner, are you?"

"Wow, is this how you are when you don't sleep for a few days?"

He ran a hand through his hair in a rough, restless gesture. "No, I'm like this because I found out that you're making secret deals with Antonio. Again."

"*Again?* What do you mean?"

"I know he's the one who put you up to marrying me."

"He told you?"

"*Si.* So tell me what are you doing meeting with him in secret in the middle of the night? Alex saw you."

"So she told on me?"

"She thought I should know that my wife is continuing negotiations with my wily grandfather, *si.* Alex despises Antonio as much as I do."

Sophia knew there was a guilty flush climbing up her cheeks. "I just… I told him to stop bullying Salvatore, and every one else, that's all. He and his gray wolf pack."

The sinuous lines of Luca's face became still. "You did?"

"Yes. It's high time someone stood up to him. He plays with everyone—Kairos, you, me, Tina. Only Leandro seems to escape his clutches. I might have gone a little overboard, I was so angry about it."

"How overboard?"

"I told him if he wasn't careful, I would send him and his pack out of the board with their tails tucked between their legs."

But Sophia had approached Antonio only to ask about Luca, for she knew Leandro could never be induced to talk about his brother. The bond between the Conti brothers, as she'd guessed, was inviolate, for all they were diametrically opposite in temperament.

What haunted Luca? Was it a medical condition? Why weren't the Contis, with all their bloody wealth, doing something to help him?

With each passing day, she felt as if she'd go mad if she didn't understand what drove Luca. It felt like an invisible wall was already pushing her away from him.

For a man who gave every outward proof of despising Luca, Antonio hadn't betrayed a single thing. Only stared at her as if she was an apparition that had appeared out of thin air. Beyond frustrated, Sophia had vented the anger, the fear that was slowly consuming her from within.

She took Luca's hand in hers, the long, elegant fingers as familiar as her own now. She'd never known this intimacy, this sort of connection with another person, in her life. Not even her mother. Somehow, Luca had become a part of her own makeup. "I would never whisper about Valentina to another soul."

"He told you about Tina?"

He sounded so disquietingly furious that the words poured out of Sophia. "I would never betray your family in that way. I would never ever pull the rug like that from anyone, much less Tina. I know what it feels like to not have a name. To not know where you belong. You believe me, don't you, Luca?"

Luca stared at Sophia, the wistfulness in her tone calming the anger inside. His grandfather really needed to keep his mouth shut. Sensing the wariness in her tense stance, he pulled her into his arms. "You fight so ferociously for Salvatore, I forget you're not even his, Sophia. Tell me more about you."

"There's not much to tell. My English father died before he could marry my mother. She became the village pariah when she found out she was pregnant. She moved to Milan to find a job and to raise me. For a long while, we struggled to make ends meet. She wasn't really suited for any kind of job. So she cleaned houses. Big, posh houses, and I tagged along whenever I could."

"It made you determined to succeed."

"Yes. I wanted to go to college, I wanted a career. Luckily for me, I did well at school. I never ever wanted to have just a glass of milk for dinner. Can you blame my fixation with cakes and pastries? Diets are torture for me, to deny myself food when we didn't have much for so long, my body revolts at the very idea."

He buried his nose in her hair, tenderness enveloping him. "Then why do you?"

"It's okay, I'm coming to realize that I'll never be stick-thin, anyway."

"You're a fighter, *cara mia*. It lights you from the inside out."

"That's what good-looking people say to the ugly ones," she retorted instantly.

They burst out laughing. She hid her face in his chest. It felt as if his lungs would burn if he even tried to contain this.

Dio, what was he going to do with this woman? She made him laugh like no one did. She cast such bright light onto everything she touched. She made him so protective of her, as if that was his only reason in the world.

She made him ache and want with a fierceness he had never known. And the days were dwindling down slowly but surely. Like sand in an hourglass. There was nothing he could do contain it. He had let her see more of him than anyone else.

Every moment he spent with her, he was living an entire lifetime in it.

Everything was becoming twisted, twined together so messily that he wasn't able to keep it separate. Different compartments for different activities, different emotions used in different places, some never to be indulged in; that was his life. There was order in his chaos.

And he didn't know how to stop it. How to harden himself against her. How to remind himself that he could not have her for more than a few weeks.

"When I was thirteen, Mom met Salvatore. He fell in love with her. I wasn't sure he'd want her with me tagging along. So I…" Her voice wavered here and suddenly, a pushing pressure came upon Luca's chest.

He stroked the tight line of her mouth. "What did you do, Sophia?"

"I decided to remove myself from the equation. I packed a bag with two pairs of clothes, took enough money for bus fare, packed two sandwiches and a banana—more than I should have, I know, but I didn't know when I would be able to eat again and I knew Sal would take care of my mom, so I ran away."

Luca's throat felt raw, imagining a barely grown girl disappearing like that. "*Christo*, Sophia! What were you thinking?"

"She needed him more than I did. I couldn't bear to see her like that anymore, shriveling to nothingness, working all hours just to get me through school."

Thirteen, she'd been only thirteen. And so brave. He didn't mistake for a second that it hadn't cost her. That it hadn't left a mark on her. That it hadn't changed her in ways even she couldn't see.

Seeing the best or worst of yourself at such a young age, it set a precedent. Now she thought it was up to her to solve her loved ones' problems.

How could Salvatore not see how precious her loyalty was? For the first time in his life, Luca offered what he always took. What he craved like he did air. Comfort, touch, companionship. That she'd revealed a part of herself, a part he was sure no one knew, made him feel as if he had gained a treasure.

Hooking his hands on her hips, he pulled her into his lap on the settee. She jerked first, as if to reject the embrace. "Sometimes, I dream the bus left with me in it."

"You're here, *tesoro*. In my arms."

Something fierce rose inside Luca. He would ensure she never had to do something like this, he promised himself, that she'd never have to sacrifice her happiness for the sake of her family. He'd look out for her.

Her thighs bracketed his as he enfolded her within his arms. He nuzzled her hair, needing to touch her as much as she needed it. Settled as she was snugly against him, it wasn't lust that she invoked in that moment. But something far more tender, and rooting.

"What happened then, *cara*?"

She inhaled noisily. "They both came after me. Mom said she didn't want a man who didn't accept me, too. Salvatore went on his knees in front of me, I mean, can you imagine the scene? Rough, abrasive Salvatore being gentle… He looked me in the eye and told me he was my father from that day. He's always been kind to me."

Luca's respect for the man rose. "Except when he arranged your marriage."

"He's traditional. He thinks women, including his shrewish daughter, need to be protected. I was ready to marry whoever he pointed at. Only the man he picked found out that I'd given up the prize to you and refused to marry me. At least, he never told Sal why." Uncertainty threaded through her tone, her soft body tense in his arms. "It was you, wasn't it? You warned them all."

Suddenly, it felt like the most important thing in the world to Luca that Sophia didn't think him cruel and heartless. Or shallow. Or a useless waste of space. Or a man who was incapable of caring. All the things he'd made himself to be became an unbearable burden when it came to her. "If I had known what Marco intended, I'd never have sent him there. I…"

That she burrowed into his arms instead of withdrawing, his breath seesawed through him. She felt like warmth and generosity, strength and softness, the woman placed in the universe, it seemed, to balance him.

Forehead tucked into his neck, she hid her face, but the quiver in her words was still there. "Why did you take part in that bet? I can't just believe you could knowingly take part in someone's humiliation. At least, tell me it was that dumb need to prove yourself among them. Tell me I was incidental, Luca and not the—"

"Hush….*cara mia*, it was nothing like that. Believe me, I…I never meant to hurt you." When she became stiff in his arms, he forced her to meet his eyes. For once in his wretched life, to show the truth, instead of hiding behind shadows. "When I heard about the bet, I was furious. But there was no way to dissuade that lot. So I joined in. Only to protect you from their stupid ploys. Instead, I got involved with you. Those weeks we spent together… It was incredible.

"But I was barely a decent man, Sophia, much less worthy of you. I had to end it. So I told them I had won the bet. Marco was supposed to see you, and then walk out quietly. But that scoundrel humiliated you. You were never supposed to know about the bet.

"When I found out what he did, I smashed his cell phone. Warned them I didn't want to hear your name again on their lips. I knew you would be cursing me to hell, which was for the best."

CHAPTER TEN

FOR A FEW SECONDS Sophia felt dazed.

He'd meant to protect her. Knowing that he'd fallen for that indescribable pull between them, she felt light. As if the invisible boulder of shame and humiliation and self-doubt she'd been carrying around her neck for a decade had been lifted away.

It didn't matter that he'd ended their relationship like that. It didn't matter that he'd run away with a lover, in an effort to sever whatever they had shared.

It only mattered that those weeks had been special to him, too.

"I did for a long time," Sophia replied. Had a woman ever been so happy to find out the real reason of why she'd been dumped? But then their whole relationship was strange. "I cursed you, and for a really crazy period there, I even considered having some voodoo done on you. You know, have your manhood shriveled or some such."

"Manhood?" he said, the word full of mockery.

She could feel her cheeks burn but for the life of her she couldn't say the *p* word. "Fine. Your instrument of pleasure."

He laughed. She loved making him laugh. It was quickly becoming the most favorite thing about herself. Second in that quickly growing list were her previously hated breasts. Anything that could fuel those dark fantasies he kept whispering in her ear proudly earned that place. "Your mighty sword? Your shaft of delight?"

Tears rolled down his cheeks and he pulled her on top of him until she was straddling him. "Say it, Sophia."

"I don't want to."

"You prude."

Her chest hurt for the laughter bursting through her. "I'm a liberated woman who has no qualms about her sexual needs. Now, go back to the house, pretty yourself up and be ready to satisfy me when I come home tonight. See?"

"You're going to pay for it."

"I'm not a prude."

"Then say it."

"Luca, that word is so clinical and dull for the fantastic, mind-blowing things you do with it. I will not call the most awesome thing in the world that horrible name."

The most debauched man on the face of the earth blushed then. His nostrils flared, his mobile mouth pursed and there was such delight in his eyes.

Sophia giggled.

He hugged her then. Tightly and like she were precious cargo. "You, *cara mia*, are going to be the death of me."

His hands reached for her shoulders again and Sophia exhaled in shuddering relief. Suddenly, she couldn't imagine going another minute without his hands on her. With urgency that was part desperation and part fear, she kissed his mouth.

"Just stay away from Antonio. And Kairos and Leandro, too, for good measure. I don't trust any of them."

"Not even your own brother, Luca?"

"Leandro will not harm you, true, but he's the master of manipulation. I don't want to take a chance."

She traced the bridge of his nose with a finger, warmth settling in all the neglected pieces of her soul. "You're doing that thing, Luca. That thing that I love you for not doing."

Luca was sure his heart had stopped for a second. "What is it?"

"Other than what you're doing now?" the minx whispered saucily against his mouth.

He laughed. "What is the other thing, then?"

"You never used to tell me what I could or should do. You only used to say *get on with it, cara mia.* Now you are like the rest of them. You want to change me."

If there was ever a warning put so perfectly, Luca didn't know what it could be. He was becoming someone else with Sophia. He had had so many lovers and he'd never been possessive of anyone.

And yet, with Sophia, the urge to protect, to possess, was primal.

He knew why, too. She made him like himself. Gave him a different definition. Beyond what he'd been predetermined by genes and history.

He saw someone else when he looked in the mirror these days. He saw the man Sophia saw. The man who evoked that slow but saucy smile when her gaze flicked to him across the boardroom, the soft flush that dusted her cheeks when he passed by and made sure he touched her amidst a crowd, the man who gave her that flushed and well-loved look when she came, the man she'd held tight when she was finally on her way to saving Rossi's from sure ruin.

The man she looked at with such fierce protectiveness when she thought he didn't know. The man she kissed when she thought he was finally asleep after seeing him walk around like a ghost. Just for her peace of mind, he'd pretended a couple of times, stayed with her until the worry for him cleared from her brow.

It was addictive, exhilarating, how she made him think of himself.

"I would never change you, Sophia. But Antonio has a habit of ruining things. And I won't always be here to shield you from him or his pack."

That was what had bothered him since Alex had told him. In his reckless need to have her, he'd made her a lot of enemies and robbed her of her one true friend.

"Then why not tell him that my advisory capacity for your stock is only temporary?"

Because he didn't mean for it to be. The idea took root, digging deep.

"Luca…"

"Now for the real reason I came here," he said, filling his hands with her breasts.

She laughed, her eyes wide, her breath already erratic. A voluptuous Venus. "Margie—"

"Margie cleverly disappeared."

"Luca…this is my first week working with members of CLG, in a new office. Your brother, your grandfather, they all work here… We can't just…"

"The question is…do you want me, *cara mia*?"

"Yes. I'm a little ashamed that I always want to say yes, Luca. It's setting a bad precedent between us, isn't it?"

"There's nothing to be ashamed about, *tesoro*. We… Our bodies were made for this…" He snuck his hands under her blouse and reached the hard tip. Lifting one lush breast, he took the nipple in his mouth through the silk of her blouse. He bit on the distended tip and suckled.

A moan fell from her throat. She muttered something filthy. He'd never been so hard and so amused at the same time.

Luca pulled her skirt up, thanked the man who invented thongs and touched her between her legs. She was utterly ready for him.

He pushed his fingers up and down the crease of her folds, played with the swollen little bud there, keenly aware of every hiss of her breath, of every shift in her body.

"Oh, Lord…" Tiny shivers shook her frame. He buried his face in one shoulder and tasted the salt of her. Sweat made her skin soft and damp.

"I wish you would say my name. It is *my* fingers

deep inside you." He hooked his fingers and swirled them in tune with his words.

She rewarded him with a groan that sent a flare of heat over every inch of him. His erection pushed against his trousers. "Oh…you…*arrogant, conceited…* Luca… I need…"

He took the tender skin between his teeth and suckled while he penetrated her lush heat with two fingers. She convulsed against him, pushing her wetness against his fingers. "What do you need, *cara mia*?"

"You. Inside me. Now."

Lifting her up, he unzipped his trousers and freed himself.

Cheeks flushed, irises dilated, wide mouth bee-stung, she took him inside her. Luca felt a deeply primal satisfaction as he glided deep into her invitingly slick heat. Like a glove, her flesh closed around him and his head went back with a groan.

Her hands in his hair, Sophia stared at him with a startling intensity.

For a few seconds, they stayed like that, unmoving, gazing into each other's eyes. Just reveling in the beauty of the moment, the raw intimacy of it.

He didn't shy away from it. Neither did she. And Luca knew it was getting out of hand. This was not merely good sex. This was not even just fantastic sex.

This was Sophia and he creating something special, something he'd never known before. The sum of them becoming more than their individual selves.

She kissed him tenderly, as if she was aware of what

the moment meant, too. As if she, too, was shaken by the wild beauty, the palpable magic of it.

And then because they were so desperate for each other, because they were greedy for what they could give each other, she moved over him.

That first slide of friction was unbearably good.

"Rotate your hips on the way down," he ordered hoarsely.

"Your wish, *my master*, is my command." Hands tight on his shoulders, she did as he said. The movement rubbed her breasts against his neck and chest, rubbed him against the slick folds of her.

"Oh, Luca…"

Loosely holding her hips, Luca let her set the pace. "I know, *cara mia*." Measly words for the fever spiraling in their blood.

Confident now, she moved faster.

Tense and fluid, demanding and supplicant. Her moans became keener, louder, signaling she was getting closer to the edge. When she arched her back on her way down, he took her mouth with his, swallowing away her cry. Not to mollify her, but because he didn't want anyone else to hear how she sounded in the throes of falling apart.

She was his, her cries, her moans, her sensual demands and her husky whimpers, *all his*.

He thrust up, fast and hard, as her muscles milked him. Climax beat at him in relentless waves, a fire breathing through his veins. Sated and in good terms with himself and the world, he wondered why in hell their marriage had to be temporary.

What was the harm in continuing like this?

They both knew what the score was. Maybe this was his chance at companionship. He was so tired of waking up with women he had no intention of knowing. Never standing still. Even if she only knew a fraction of him, it was still more than anyone else did.

He pushed damp hair away from her forehead and pressed his lips to her temple. She snuggled against him, and Luca, for the first time in his place, felt completely at peace with himself.

CHAPTER ELEVEN

SOPHIA WOKE UP with a start, something sinuously haunting seemed to have lodged in her veins, and peered at the unfamiliar surroundings. This was not the high, luxurious bed that she had taken to falling into in exhaustion the past month. The walls were not the pale cream, the drapes not the sunny yellow that Luca pulled away a couple of times, calling her a lazy cat. No great Conti wealth peered down from paintings on walls.

This was not the bedroom in Villa de Conti where Luca had joined her at all hours of the night in the past month—once it had been 3:00 a.m. and she wasn't sure who was more shocked, she, to see him emerge buck naked and dripping wet from the shower, or he, to see her sneak into the bedroom with her laptop and a sliver of red velvet cake from his niece Izzie's birthday party.

What had followed had been a crazy night of cake, champagne, a wet Luca and the bed.

Here, the walls were bare and the general impression of the room was utter chaos. The bed on which she lay was the only surface not covered in books and loose paper. Realization came slowly to her sore, sated body—this was Luca's studio. The only familiar thing here was the unmistakable scent that their bodies created together—the scent of sex and sweat and raw intimacy.

When she hadn't seen Luca in a week, nor heard a word, she'd invaded Leandro's office, demanding to know where Luca was. With each passing day that she hadn't seen him, a frenzy of fear and worry had built inside her.

Kairos had been defeated in his pursuit to be CEO of CLG, leaving the position empty, and wouldn't even talk to her. Rossi's financial future looked better than it had in a decade. And Luca had thoroughly ravished her, his eagerness and passion chasing away her own inhibitions, not that she'd need much persuading once she'd seen past his facade.

Now that all his goals had been achieved, was he done with their marriage? The memory of how easily he'd walked away last time—whatever the reason—wouldn't leave her alone.

This time, she wanted him to say to it to her face.

She wanted closure if he was ending this. But more than that, she had enough of the game he played with the world. She wanted to face the real Luca. She wanted the truth of him, a part of him that no one else knew before she let him finish this.

Grudgingly, and with warnings, Leandro had driven her to the high-rise building that was only a few miles from the Conti offices. He'd accompanied her to the door.

If Luca had been shocked to see her standing on the threshold of his apparently inviolate space, he'd hidden it quite thoroughly. Naked torso and blue jeans molded to hard thighs, he'd sent her heart thudding. Dark hair all kinds of rumpled and a gaunt, introspective set to his features that she'd come to recognize as a need for solitude, he looked utterly delectable.

Arms folded, Leandro waited and watched them, a faint tension emanating from him. He didn't know what Luca was going to do. With her, she'd realized with a sliver of alarm running up her spine.

But even the thought that Luca could harm her was ludicrous. Strip her armor and distill her to the core of her, yes. Hurt her with reckless or cruel intent, no. She was as sure as the wild beat of her heart in her chest, like the flutter of a trapped bird.

"Hello, Bluebeard," she'd tossed at Luca then with a manufactured sauciness, and ducked under his arm, refusing to give him a chance to turn her away.

She didn't care that he hadn't even sent her one of his teasing, quirky texts in a week. That he didn't want her infiltrating whatever it was that he guarded so fiercely. She didn't care that in a matter of weeks he wouldn't want her in his life.

Already, there were warning signs. At least once every day, he reminded her the days were counting down, a calculating look in his eyes. Afraid that that one question would start a conversation she was in no way prepared for, she'd evaded him. She didn't care that slowly her heart, her emotions, her very soul, were slipping away from her. That she had lost all rationality about this thing between them. That for the first time in her life, it wasn't her career or her family's future keeping her up at night.

That had been at seven in the evening. He'd closed the door and turned to look at her, a devouring light in his eyes. Slowly relief gave way to other uncomfortable emotions—awkwardness and anxiety. They stood there staring at each other, both aware that a line had been crossed.

She didn't say, *you didn't call in six days*.

He didn't say, *you're acting like a clingy wife*.

When he reached her and cupped her jaw, she'd almost wept with relief. "You look exhausted."

She'd leaned into his touch, too far gone to even think of hiding her need for him. "Didn't sleep much the last few days. I don't know how you do this all the time."

His fingers covered her nape; his nose rubbed against her jaw. "How did your proposal go?"

She smiled against his shoulder, the familiar scent of sweat and soap and skin anchoring her. "It went very well." Nuzzling into his skin, feeling the thud of his heart under her hands, only then did the clamor in her blood calm. "With you on my side, I can even achieve world domination."

"Bene."

He'd picked her up then, as if she weighed nothing, and declared they'd go to bed. For sleep, first, and then other things that they both were in desperate need of, he'd declared throatily against her hair.

The scrape of her skin against the soft cotton told

her she was still utterly naked. Instinctively, she pulled the duvet up toward her chin and turned to her side.

The pillow didn't even bear an indentation—he hadn't slept at all. Whereas she'd been thoroughly wiped out. Like a possessed man, he'd driven her to the edge again and again. He'd always been playful before, even when he'd made her do the wickedest things.

Laughter colored everything they did. Even when they were hungrily going at each other like rabbits. He said the funniest things and found her no-nonsense outlook humorous. Except tonight.

A price, he'd said, scratching his stubble against the tender skin of her inner thigh, when she'd begged him to stop. She had to pay a price for coming to Bluebeard's lair. And even with his wicked mouth at the core of her, and her throat raw from screaming his name, Sophia realized she'd already paid a price.

A crisp breeze flew in and she shivered, the last remnants of sleep chased away. Her eyes adjusted to the darkness punctured by the moonlight through the floor-to-ceiling glass doors. Wrapping the sheet around her, she walked to them and peered through.

It was pitch-black, the darkest time of the night, just before dawn.

She went into the bathroom, washed her face. Sneaking into his closet, she found a dress shirt and pulled it on over her underwear.

That was when she heard it.

The strains of music. That same tune he'd played haltingly, almost lazily, that night of the party. *It* had woken her.

Heart beating a thousand times faster, she went, her entire being tugged as if by a rope. Just as she reached the door and pushed it open, the music stopped.

No, no, no.

Like a wisp of smoke she'd been chasing for hours in some deep, dark forest but forever lost now. Only an echo of it lingered, in the very stillness of the air, in the loud thud of her heart.

"Play it again," she demanded, leaning against the wall, her voice loud and uneven.

Skin stretched taut to stiffness over muscle, his bare back was a map to his mood. His hands still on the keys, he didn't turn around. "I didn't realize you were awake."

Sophia walked a couple more steps into the room and halted. An urgency was building in her, as if she was at a crossroads that would change her life. "You gave it your best shot to wear me out, I know. What did you think to do once I fell asleep? Smuggle me out of here? Drug me and take me back?" For the life of her she couldn't keep the accusation out of her tone. "Even you, with your unending energy and libido, can't keep me in that room forever."

He turned and leveled a look at her over his shoulder. "You're developing a sense for drama."

"Dramas and masks are your forte."

He raised a brow then. Masculine arrogance dripped from the lazy gesture. Her breath held, Sophia waited, for he could rip her apart in that moment. It was the same look he'd worn when she'd said he thrived on control. He would have decimated her then, too, but

Sophia had backed off. Stalled him by offering herself up.

Only a few steps between them but it could have been an oceans-wide chasm. A stranger looked back at her. Not the one who laughed with her. Not the one who'd moved inside her like he was an extension of her own body.

She stayed at the door, afraid of breaking whatever tenuous thing had built between them. Afraid that if she walked out the door tonight, it was all over.

"Please… Only once. I…would give anything you ask of me to hear it once."

Something akin to shock flashed in his eyes.

She forced herself to smile, to act as if her heart wasn't rearing to leap out of her chest. As if she weren't standing over some abyss, ready to fall in. Fear and hope twisted into a rope in her belly.

"I…have never played for anyone. Not even Leandro and Tina."

"I don't give a damn. I want to hear it."

He didn't blink at her outburst. He didn't reply. He just turned back to the piano. Silence reigned for so long that Sophia was sure she had lost.

But then long fingers moved on the keys. The tension melted from his shoulders and back. He became fluid, an extension of the instrument. He forgot her, Sophia realized. There was no one but him and the tune that flew from his fingers.

Slow, haunting, full of a soul-deep pain. It continued like that, sneaking insidiously into every pore, every cell, until Sophia felt the haunting desperation as her own. It was gut-wrenching, visceral, with a swirling motif turning back on itself again and again, as if it couldn't free itself of its tethers. As if it was choking but still couldn't escape.

Until a different note emerged and almost disappeared. She tensed, wondering if she was imagining it. If it was her own audacious hope that she was hearing in the music.

But that note emerged again, like the crest of a wave, like the brilliance of light in a darkened corner. Again and again, until the haunting pain was slowly being washed away by the tremulous hope. The tempo picked up, now the notes of pain and fear being lost among the high notes. It rose and rose until nothing but hope remained. Even that hope was tentative, fragile, a jaggedly painful life but still it glittered.

The high note held and held until it soared like a bird in the sky, stretching every nerve in her tight.

Sophia sank to the floor, her body shuddering at an avalanche of emotions she couldn't even name. Her knees and hands shook, tears running a blistering path over her cheeks.

She felt transformed, like she herself had risen from the ashes, painfully new but full of hope. The beauty of the composition was an ache in her throat. For several minutes—or was it aeons?—she stayed there on the floor, her heart too full to feel anything.

Slowly, her heartbeat returned to normal and the contrast of the silence that descended was deafening. Like the silence a storm left after its destruction.

Luca stayed at the piano. She'd never seen him so

remote, so distant, almost as if he stood at the edge of civilization instead of being the charming lover pursued in droves by women.

She pushed herself to her feet. Today she would heed his unspoken warning for she felt like a leaf that could be blown away by the wind. She couldn't laugh if he told some slick joke. She couldn't bear it if he became that…that travesty of an indulgent playboy when that astonishing beauty, that incredible music, resided in him.

For once, she didn't feel victorious for being right. She felt nauseous and furious and frayed at the edges.

"What did you think of it, Sophia?"

His question stilled her hand on the door. She looked at the dark oak, unwilling to face him. How could he contain so much inside himself? How had he bared a part of him but ripped away something of her?

"It was…interesting," she replied. There was no word that could do justice to that piece of music. All she knew was that she needed to get away from him before she did something stupid like bawl over him… or rage at him with her fists. Was this what came out of those periods of restlessness, those times that he disappeared?

It was like that piece of music had broken open the cupboard in her head and all she could see, feel, were messy emotions roiling in and out of her. She was spoiling for a fight, a down and dirty match. She felt a huge wave of emotion building inside her, battering at her to burst out.

"Interesting?" he said, and she heard a sliver of laughter in that single word. "I think that's the first diplomatic thing I've ever heard you say."

She turned and faced him.

He looked like the same Luca who'd mocked her three hours ago. The same one who had fed her strawberries and cream while she'd worked on her laptop, the same one who'd brought her pots of tea and pastries when she'd worked into dawn. The same man who had licked and stroked her to ecstasy as if it were the one and only reason he was put on the planet.

But he wasn't the same.

She didn't know him at all.

Slowly, she realized what he was telling her. What his slick smile was about—an invitation to join him in the parody he carried out every day. Nausea welled up inside her.

"Whose composition is it?" she asked, giving him a chance, giving him a warning of her own. "It sounds... classical."

He smiled then. And instead of charm, she saw condescension. Instead of genuine amusement, she saw smugly bored arrogance. Instead of miles of charm and insouciant wit and reckless antics, she saw pain and utter anguish and a thin flicker of hope. Instead of a man who went through life in pursuit of reckless pleasure, she saw a brooding, dark stranger.

Like she was at a reproduction of Dr. Jekyll and Mr. Hyde.

"Do you know classical music, then?"

Look at them, holding a conversation as if they were

on a first date. Thrusting and deflecting as if there wasn't a storm gathering around them.

She shrugged, preparing herself for the fight. He knew nothing of her if he thought she would back down now. "There were a few months there after my mom and Sal married where he thought I required a little polish. It was a bleak time. There was a piano teacher, ballet classes and even an art teacher. Penguin me and ballet, can you imagine?"

"If you call yourself a penguin one more time, I shall spank you."

"I also now see why Tina was so amused when I called you a peacock."

"What am I, then?"

"A panther."

"Why?"

"Its spots are in plain sight under that black coat. It is more vulnerable than any other jungle cat for, however much it tries, it can't blend in like the other ones. It automatically stands out."

He stood like a statue, with his hands behind him. The man she had thought couldn't be still in any way, the man she'd thought lacked any depth. What a laugh he must have had all this time…

"But we were talking about music, weren't we? I practiced for hours and hours, determined to be the perfect little princess to please Sal. Even though my strength lay in numbers. Mr. Cavalli said I was brilliant with technique, but I played without soul. That for me it was just a means to an end." How right old Mr. Cavalli had been.

Music, music like Luca played, just was. It defied paltry human parameters. It defied night and day; it defied constriction or boundaries. It defied definition of any sort.

"Like a piece of flaky, buttery pastry, he'd say, only without the warm, sugary goodness in the middle. It was such a good metaphor, I was completely horrified and quit. So, yeah…I do know a bit about music."

And before she could regulate the words, they shot out. Like pieces of jagged rocks shattering the carefully constructed glass wall around him. "It's yours, isn't it, Luca? You wrote that piece."

CHAPTER TWELVE

THEY'D HAD SO LITTLE time left. A handful of moments. Of laughter and making love. Of late-night feasts and frantic early-morning sex. He was going to pack so many things into that time. He was going to persuade her the best way he knew to extend the duration of their marriage.

To however long it would take for them to get each other out of their systems.

Now they had nothing.

It was over.

Luca felt a strange kind of relief on one side. That it was all over. The end of things was something he was infinitely familiar and comfortable with.

Hiding in plain sight had never been harder than it was with Sophia. She clawed and ripped, cajoled and kissed her way to the core of him. The rational part of him that reminded him whose son he was and how he had come to be took a beating at her hands.

You are Luca Conti, it shouted in an eternally tireless voice, forever reminding him what he should and shouldn't have. It grounded him. It balanced him.

Then there was the second half. The part that he had never made peace with. The part that craved and gobbled up everything and anything, that demystified the most complex puzzles for him in a matter of seconds.

He'd always thought of it as a yawning blackness, forever hungry.

There was beauty in it; there was intellect in it. And above all, it just was.

And it was that part that was thrashing, wild with grief, already mourning the loss of this woman. The woman who above everyone else had seen and identified it. The woman who promised friendship, companionship, acceptance with her words and demands.

But Luca had a lifetime of practice suppressing this part of him. Or at least ignoring it just enough. Pretending that it didn't exist had only pushed him even more toward the edge. Like Antonio had done with his father.

So instead, he had compartmentalized it. Like a wild dog that was fed just enough from time to time to keep it compliant, to keep it tethered.

He felt Sophia's hand on his flesh and realized how cold he was. Or maybe that was grief, too.

"Luca?"

Turning toward her fully, he answered her. "It is my own. I finished it this last week. Which is why I didn't call you."

Her beautifully intelligent eyes flared then steadied. "A week?"

"*Si.*"

"You don't sleep or stop until you finish it."

He shrugged.

Now the truth lay between them, a dark specter.

He could see that she hadn't expected him to agree. She had guessed it but there had been a small hope that it might not be true. That he was the waste of space she thought him rather than...*whatever freak of nature* he was. It was the same realization he had seen in his mama's eyes for years before she'd left.

The tremulous hope that his last episode of restlessness and headaches and the furiously written music was all just a one off. And the crushing sense of defeat as she realized that he was just like his father. Not just in form but in his mind, too.

As if that wasn't unbearable enough for her.

With Sophia, however, that bucking lasted only a few seconds. He saw, with a strangely detached fascination, the moment she faced the disconcerting truth and accepted it. Her shoulders squared. Stubborn chin lifted, ready to march into battle.

He laughed then. And because he was so weak, and because he had trapped himself without a way out, he hauled her toward him and kissed her. He, the creative genius with an IQ off the charts, he had thought himself so clever. He would seduce her, he would steal a part of her and then go on his merry way. Or he would take and take of her but give nothing of his own self.

What an arrogant fool he was...

At the back of his mind, furious panic was setting in. Like a gathering wave of blackness that would rip him apart. It sent his heart thudding so loud that he could feel it in his throat.

His lips on Sophia's became more demanding, rough, desperate. He wanted to sink under her skin and never emerge. He wanted to drown in her forever. He'd barely breathed the pure, shining wonder that was she before she pushed him away. Wiped her mouth with the back of her hand.

"Is my touch already that distasteful, *cara mia*?" he retorted, unable to keep the ugly jeer out of his tone. Unable to not slide a little into the quagmire of self-pity.

This was what happened when he forgot who and what he was. *Dio*, he became a wounded, raving dog. And if she didn't leave soon, he would take a chunk out of her.

"What?" She glared at him first. Then her eyes lost that glazed look, her mouth became a purse of displeasure and then she shook her head at him. "You kiss me and I lose all rationality, all common sense. I will not let you sex me up and send me on my way again, with a pat and an orgasm."

Something in him calmed at the matter-of-fact tone. As long as she didn't loathe him, he could still keep his dignity even as he ended the one meaningful relationship of his life. He sighed, folded his hands and leaned against the wall. He would last through this, too. He always did. "Sophia, you are making a big—"

"You cheated me, again. You—"

He laughed. "Even you couldn't rise above making this about you, could you?"

She flushed. "I was just warming up. Your entire life is a lie."

A shaft of anger pierced him and he welcomed it. He never lost his temper, as a rule. There was enough unpredictability in his head and he ruled the rest of it with a tight leash. Trust Sophia to provoke that, too. "My life is what I need it to be."

"And why is that? This is not the dark ages to fear… talent, *no…talent* is such a lukewarm word, isn't it?" Her entire body bristled with the force of her words. "To fear such beauty, such…genius, whatever else it is accompanied by. You can't just…throw it away like this. My God, what is your brother thinking?"

His faith in her wavered then, at the strange light in her eyes. "My brother thinks I have enough problems to deal with without pursuing fame and recognition."

"Fame and recognition, Luca? That's not what I mean. There is such beauty in your music, such pain and hope…" Tears filled her eyes and swept down. "I…I just wish… Looking at you, at the perfect foil your looks and your charm provide you, I can hardly believe it.

"Until I close my eyes and that music moves through me. Then I open my eyes and I see you. All of you."

The sight of Sophia's tears unmanned him like nothing else.

"Why have you made your life into such a travesty? How can you bear to contain all that and breeze through life as if you were nothing? You have made a joke out of a gift—"

It came at him then, fraying the edges of his temper. Anger and self-loathing and utter helplessness. He stepped away from her. It was the helplessness that flayed him. Always. And he knew Sophia wouldn't stop until he laid himself bare in front of her. Until he stood there in all his utterly powerless nakedness. Until he satisfied her, too, that this was all he could be.

"I've never had a choice to be anything else. I do not believe it is a gift."

He saw her blanch then. "The headaches and the insomnia… I'm sure they make it very hard. But you said yourself—"

"You're not listening, Sophia. My father was like this but violent. Antonio neither helped him nor controlled him, with the fear of the Conti name being dragged through mud. Enzo ran wild, buried those headaches in alcohol and drugs. He became abusive. And when my mother told him she was leaving him, he…lost it. He…" His voice broke here, and Luca felt like he was a jagged rock, full of painful edges, never changing. "He forced himself on her. And you know what she had as a result? Me, in his image, every which way."

There it was, his shame. The very cause of his existence. A mass of ugliness shrieking in the room with them.

Acid burned through his throat. He wanted to sink to his knees and cry as he'd done the day he'd found out. He wanted to throw himself into her arms as he'd done once with his brother. He wanted to…take Sophia and bury himself in her sweetness; he wanted to escape in her arms one more time.

But he would not give in to any of those urges.

To not rail at something he could not change, to not become what his father had, that was in his hands. It was his choice to make.

So he stood there, bending and bucking at the fresh grief that tore through him with vicious claws, but refusing to break. For it had been years since he had felt the loss of the freedom to be anything else. But she made the grief and the loss fresh tonight.

Sophia made everything hurt again, ravage him. Everything was excruciatingly raw again.

Her face had lost all its color; tears filled her eyes and overflowed. Luca held her gaze, locked away his own. Crying had ever only made his headaches worse and all his pain was reflected in her clear gaze, anyway.

She didn't utter platitudes. She just stood there unflinching, absorbing everything he threw at her. As if his pain was hers. As if she would stand and fight for him, too. As if he, too, had been accepted into that band of people she loved and protected so fiercely... He had never wanted to belong to someone as desperately as he did then. Never wanted to put himself in another's hands so much.

He never wanted to believe that he could have loved so much.

He weakened then. Almost broke. Until he started speaking again, until he reminded himself. "He was a monster to her. And every time she looked at me, *Mama* broke inside a little. And then I started having these bouts of restlessness, these...episodes. In the beginning, I was barely rational through them. They terrified her. *I terrified her.* In the end, she walked out. So do not dare to tell me that it is a gift I should celebrate or rejoice. Or share with others. Do not presume to tell me how I should live my life."

He thought he was like his father. That wasn't just Antonio's fear.

It was Luca's, too.

But Luca, unlike half the thickheaded men she knew, was also extremely self-aware, was so much in touch with his emotions. He had to know he was nothing like his father. That he would never hurt anyone.

"Did you ever get violent like him?" she asked, still processing everything he'd told her. He looked remote, painfully alone. This was his cross to bear, she could see. This fear was the invisible wall she'd been throwing herself against.

He shook his head. "No. I… When I was too young to understand, Antonio thought I was just being a boy. But my brother, he understood it. He would never leave me alone, night or day through it. Headaches, or insomnia, or madly scribbling notes on paper, Leandro stayed with me like a shadow. He…helped me develop self-discipline, told me again and again that just because I was a genius that didn't mean he would be my servant. But he became more—he became mother and father and friend to me."

Sophia smiled and nodded, a little of the pressure in her chest relieving. She would kiss Leandro when she saw him next for what he had done for Luca. But there was also panic building inside her. A sense of cavernous loss and a chasm of distance between her and Luca that she couldn't cross. "Then you're nothing like him, are you?" She heard the crack in her tone then. The desperation.

But none of it touched him. "You're a foolish woman if you think I'm not. After everything I just told you."

Standing helplessly there, Sophia realized it then.

That he was like his father was not a fear. It had become his shield against more hurt. More rejection. It was his reason to separate himself from everyone, his reason to loathe himself.

What else could a mere boy do to protect himself against the violent image that he'd been brought into life through such a horrible act? Against a fate he couldn't change? And what torture to be always reminded of it, again and again, of the man who'd wreaked that destruction, to have no escape from it?

Something so beautiful, but tainted in ugliness. Much as she pitied his mother, Sophia was filled with a powerless rage. "She should have protected you. It was not your burden to bear."

For it was nothing but a burden. An unimaginable one. Every inch of her flinched when she imagined how trapped he must feel always. How much he must crave escape from himself…

"How can you blame her of all people?" He was blazingly furious now. But Sophia much preferred him like this instead of that cold smile he'd given her earlier. She preferred the wild, unruly part of him, the part she was sure he hated. "She was innocent in all this."

"So were you!" she yelled, fresh tears pouring out of her eyes. "She could've been stronger for you. She… It was not your fault. None of this is."

"I'm aware of that. You think I have been punishing myself all these years? Do you see the life I have lived?"

She wiped her cheeks and smiled. "No, and I think that is your greatest accomplishment, isn't it? Not that beautiful piece of music. Not whatever mysteries your genius mind can solve. Not the big joke you play on the whole world. You laugh through life, you strut through it, you don't make any apologies for the way you do it…" She was laughing a little and crying a little again. "You…*live it so gloriously, Luca.*"

Her chest constricted, every inch of her yearning to hold him to her, to mold him with her fingers. To feel that hard body against hers and tell him that he was loved. That he was the most glorious, wonderful man she'd ever met. That he'd filled her life with courage, and laughter and love these past months.

That he was better, more than any man she'd ever known.

Genius or not, Luca was generous, kind, magnificent. But now that she knew the reality of him, now that she had heard his music, there was no escape. Her fate was tied to his.

She had toppled into love and it was exactly as she had feared. Her knees were skinned, her body bruised, her heart already taking a beating. And after all her careful maneuvering through it, after being strong for so many years, he was going to rip apart the very fabric of her life.

For there was no light in her world without him. No laughter, no joy, no color. She was nothing but the drab, colorless, staid Sophia.

His poisonous hatred about his genius, his self-loathing, it all stood there like a dark, forbidding stone wall that she couldn't climb, much less conquer. An almost tangible thing rushing him away from her, blocking her. "You live this life you've been given, Luca. I can't help but admire that."

Something flashed in his face then—relief or peace—and she thought it might be a small chink in his armor. A tiny crack in that impenetrable wall. "Then we are in agreement, *si*? Because I thought we could make this a more permanent arrangement. With some ground conditions."

The offer was made with a tease, a lighthearted tone. But it was full of wretchedness, too. For he also knew what it meant if she hated the other part of him. If she agreed it was a shame to be hidden away because now she knew where it came from.

She could see it all in his face, she understood his complex mind so well. Not now, but eventually, he would hate her a little for what he was already doing, too.

She was damned if she did and damned if she didn't. Despair gave way to anger. How dare he decide their fate like this? Who had given him this right to govern her joy? "No, we're not in agreement. I will not hate, I *can't* hate something that is part of you. Like you do. I won't pretend. I can't look at you and not see all of you. The masks have come off—there's no going back, Luca."

"I didn't realize you have a love for such melodrama."

"Drama? You think I choose this any more than you choose to be what you are? I accept the part of you that flitted from woman to woman all these years because you thought that was the only kind of connection you could have. So I must accept this, too. Please, Luca." She reached for him then. "Don't you see I understand?"

He stiffened, his features haunted. Pain was a live thing in his eyes then. "You see me as broken now, and I can't stand it. I have never pitied myself and neither will you."

Her own fury rose, fueled by fear. Why wasn't he seeing what he meant to her? She wasn't the sentimental sort; she didn't know how to make big declarations. She didn't even understand half of the riotous emotions coursing through her right then. All she knew was this: they could not end that night, not over this. "Do not presume to tell me what I feel about you, then."

"I have given you everything I'm capable of, everything I have, Sophia."

"I have found that place, Luca, the place where I want to dwell. By your side. Just don't ask me to pretend like I don't know the true you now. I can't unsee you. I can't unhear that music…" But even as she said it, she knew nothing would change his mind.

His beliefs about himself were bone-deep, a disease that would steal him away from her. He would never accept himself. And he would never accept what she felt for him.

He had not left her with an illusion of her strength, either; he'd left her nowhere to hide. Reckless, he'd ripped it all from her and now she had nothing to fight him with.

Such powerlessness flew through Sophia's veins that she wanted to throw something at the wall. She wanted to beat her fists into something and feel the crunch of bones.

But she did nothing like that. Sensible as always, she realized the futility of a violent tantrum. There was nothing to do but wait and hope that he would let her in again. That years of deeply held self-belief might shift.

She reached him and laid her hands on his shoulders. Her fingers moved over the slopes of his neck, the jut of his collarbone, the warm, taut stretch of skin over muscle.

He didn't reject her touch. He didn't return it, either. The man who always, *always*, touched her as if he couldn't bear it otherwise, who had taught her what it was to touch and kiss and learn another, didn't touch her now.

Head bowed, he stood there like a statue, a warm, wonderful man who'd all but ripped a vital part of himself and kept it away.

She kissed first one cheek and then the other. Masculine and sweaty, the scent of him made her blood sing. The clench of his muscles as she wrapped her arms around his naked back… She was aware of every breath in him as if it were her own. Finally, she clasped his cheek and kissed his mouth. Poured every bit of her into that kiss. "If only you would give me one chance—yourself, one chance—Luca. Give this thing between us one chance…"

Sophia turned and left his studio. His world. And a huge part of herself with him.

It took Sophia three weeks and a clip of Luca dancing with a seminaked burlesque dancer in a night club in Paris—circulated by Marco Sorcelini—to realize Luca wasn't coming back.

When she'd discovered from Leandro that Luca had left not just Milan, but Italy, the morning after that painful night, something inside her had frozen. She had packed it all away, told herself that he needed time to figure it out, to stop running. After all, the fear that he could be like his father, the ugly truth that he should have never had to face, that isolated lifestyle he'd made into an art form, had a decades-deep grip on him.

It had been his shield against more rejection, against pain.

How could he let go of those beliefs just for her? How could she expect him to, after knowing her for only a few months?

Interestingly, it was a discussion prompted by her stepfather that had torn the blinders from her eyes.

Sophia had returned from work at almost eleven

when she'd seen Salvatore waiting for her in the study. Knowing that she couldn't indefinitely avoid her parents' concern, she'd joined him. She was exhausted, sleep-deprived and she'd caught the first hint of the rumors about her record short marriage.

No one woman could keep the Conti Devil...

Conti Devil seeking new distractions...

Conti Devil flees Italy and his marriage...

Her cheeks hurt from the number of times she'd tried to keep her expression calm.

Salvatore offered her a glass of water and peered at her patiently while she finished it off. "Sophia, have you decided what you're going to do?"

"About what, Sal?"

His dark brows had gathered into a frown. "About your marriage. I think it is better for you and Rossi's if we see a lawyer immediately. Now, I have—"

Wretched fury burst out of Sophia. Her whole adult life, it was all she'd heard about—the Rossi Glory, the Rossi Legacy. "Is Rossi's all you care about?"

Salvatore blanched. "*Non.* I worry about you, too, Sophia. But after years, Rossi's is benefitting from the Conti family's influence and it is better to separate your marriage from the business as—"

"Christ, Sal! Rossi's is not thriving because of Leandro or Luca or the great CLG. But because of me! I'm the one who turned the company around. I'm the one who..." Shameful tears blocked her throat; Sophia looked away from him. But the tears had also released her fear.

She had had enough of lying down and taking what

she was given. Tired of fighting for a place without actually demanding her due. Like a faithful dog happy with scraps.

That infuriatingly slick charmer had been right in this, too.

Looking thoroughly befuddled, Salvatore took her hand in his. "I have loved you like you were my own—"

The dam broken, Sophia snatched her hand away. Words were so easy. Staying behind lines, worrying about Sal's fears, justifying Luca's past as reason enough for his current cowardice... It was all so easy. "Do you truly, Sal? Then why not trust me with your great Rossi legacy? Why have you never considered me to be your successor? After all, I've worked damned hard to be here. I'm the best thing that's happened to the company in years."

And just like that, Sophia fought her own insecurities, ripped away the cocoon of self-delusion she'd built for herself. Even then, guilt about her family and her love for this abrasive but inherently kind man almost took her out at the knees. "I have only ever worked to make Rossi's whole again. It is my company as much as it is yours. But unless you see that, unless you give me the role I deserve, I quit, Sal. Tonight, now. Consider this my official resignation."

Sophia had barely turned around when Sal stopped her. Her tears ran down her cheeks, a testament to what the cruel Luca Conti had done to her again.

Hands on her shoulders, Sal lifted her chin, quite like he had done when she had been thirteen. Black eyes filled with regret and concern and a gruff sort of tenderness. "You will forgive an old man his old prejudices, *si*, Sophia? You are right. You are and have always been stronger than any son I hoped for. Rossi Leather and its future, they are all tied to you. You are its future, *bella*. Forgive me, *si*?"

When he pulled her into his warm embrace, Sophia broke down into shuddering sobs. She cried for herself and for Luca, wondered if he would ever come back.

That night, desperate for a little connection to him, Sophia packed a bag and went back to Villa de Conti at the stroke of midnight. If Leandro and Tina thought her a little mad, they didn't betray it by word or look. Her throat had filled with tears when they had silently stood in support while she wandered through Luca's room like a wraith.

He'd given her everything—a chance to save Rossi's, an opportunity to explore her potential, a new family that somehow seemed to love wholeheartedly despite their differences, and more important than anything else, her belief in herself.

What was she supposed to do with all the riches in the world when he wasn't there? What was pride when her heart itself was broken?

She lay awake in the bed she'd shared with Luca countless times and cried again. It was time to face another truth.

Her foolish belief to wait and hope that Luca would let her in again was nothing but sheer cowardice. The deep freeze that seemed to have settled around her heart ever since that night, her self-possession, her brittle calmness in the face of the rumors flying about Luca dumping her after three months of marriage was nothing but docile acceptance of his decision. A habit that was as embedded in her, it seemed, just as Luca's fear was.

Instead of fighting and scratching and kicking her way into his life, she hid beneath her fake strength. She had even started withdrawing from society, afraid of facing their pity, or scorn or both.

She'd done this the last time, too. Instead of confronting him, she'd quietly slipped back to her life, accepting his decision. Not this time.

Not when she knew that the kind of intimacy and connection and laughter that she and Luca had shared came once in a lifetime. Not when she knew they were made for each other. Not when there was so much love to be filled in both their lives if only…

If she had to break Luca to make him face himself, face Sophia and her love, she'd do it. If it was destruction he wanted, she would hand it to him. She would shatter every pretense he'd carried out, rip apart every lie he'd weaved around himself.

And maybe when there was an end to all the things he clung to, an end to the farce, an end to life as he knew it, maybe then they could have a new beginning.

But one thing was sure: she wasn't giving up without a fight.

CHAPTER THIRTEEN

Two months later

LUCA WALKED INTO the high-ceilinged breakfast room of Villa de Conti and stilled. Shock rippled through the room, a tangible tension in the air. His family looked up at him—relief the more prevalent of emotions flitting across their faces.

"Where the hell were you?" Leandro shouted across the vast room, his legendary self-control absent. "*Dio*, Luca! You could've been be lying dead in some part of the world for all we knew."

"*Papa*, you're shouting and swearing," Luca's seven-year-old niece, Izzie, piped up.

Luca raised a brow at his brother. "If I die, you would hear."

"We know you're not dead." This was Tina. "You made sure we all knew what you were up to."

Something in her gaze caught Luca and for once in his life, he shied away from his little sister. Had he changed or she?

Izzie lifted her arms to him. "I missed you, *Zio*."

Here was another one of the female variety from whom he'd never been able to hide. He lifted her from the breakfast chair and buried his face in her sweet, strawberry-scented hair. Something loosened in his gut.

Small arms clutched his neck tightly. He pulled her tiny hands from around his neck, kissed her cheek and put her back in her chair.

His sister-in-law, Alex, was next. Usually, Alex, who was slender and willowy, coming at him was like holding a bouquet of dainty summer flowers. Pleasant and leaving him with an utter sense of well-being, of deep, unwavering affection. Of the innate goodness of life.

Heavy with pregnancy, when she threw herself at him today, though, Luca wavered on his feet and smiled. Her grip was just as tight as her daughter's around his neck. "You worried the hell out of all of us. Are you well, Luca?"

A lump lodged in his throat and he nodded.

What a fool he'd been... He'd denied a part of himself for so many years. And in the process, denied himself so many good things, too. He kissed Alex's cheek soundly, knowing it irritated Leandro. "You still won't run away and marry me, *cara*?" He said it loudly and saw the scowl on his brother's face.

Alex pulled back from his arms, ran a shaking hand over his cheek and laughed. "Bigamy, I believe, is a crime in Italy, too, isn't it?"

And just like that, the pressure on his chest returned.

Dio, he felt like he walked around with a permanent boulder on his chest. Or he was developing some serious heart trouble. Personally, he preferred the second. At least he could get it treated.

But no such luck.

He was in the peak of his prime, a physically perfect specimen of mankind. Although, lately, he'd begun to loathe himself less for what was inside, too.

He kissed Tina's cheeks, leveled a cursory nod at Antonio and sat down.

The scent of coffee and pastries filled the air, the tinkle of coffee cups and cutlery discordant in the awkward silence. Izzie finished her milk and toast, hugged him again, sought reassurance that he wouldn't disappear again and left the room.

Luca waited, his breath pent up in his chest, his fingers not quite steady.

They were looking at him, and then shying away. He put his coffee cup down so hard that half the coffee sloshed over his fingers. "I haven't gone mad, so everybody can breathe easier." Only the frown on Antonio's face relaxed.

He had to give his dear old *Nonno* some points for constancy—always a little afraid for Luca.

Leandro shrugged. "I never thought you would."

All his brother had ever done was tell Luca that he had a choice to be like their father or not. But Sophia had showed him that the choice was not just to be different from his father. But he had the choice of accepting himself, too. Of being happy in his own skin.

"Destroy every chance at any happiness you could

have, like I almost did? *Si*," Leandro continued. "Fall into some kind of mad abyss and froth at the mouth? *Non*.

"What Enzo did or was, what resides in you, that is not our legacy, Luca. What we do with our lives, is. Aren't you the one who told me that?"

His throat full of unshed tears, Luca nodded. And then he asked the question that had been tormenting him all the way through his trek through the markets in Marrakesh. Through the deserts of the Middle East and the cold winter of Prague.

Through endless parties and long lonely nights even in the midst of crowds. Because Sophia was right. His mask was off and he was tired of pretending that he was worthless. He was tired of acting as if what he had was enough.

For years he'd made an art form of running away from himself. But he couldn't run away from Sophia and his thoughts of her. He couldn't run away from the man she made him to be, the man she thought him to be.

"How is she?"

There, he was bare naked again. With no place to hide, no mask in place to retreat behind if it hurt. No shallow facade to reject before being rejected. It was not a feeling he was going to get used to anytime soon.

"Ask her when you see her."

"Why am I seeing her?" He wanted to, desperately. But for once in his life, he didn't know what he was going to say. All his charm, his quicksilver mind, nothing really helped when he lay awake for long hours wondering what he would say to her.

How he would beg.

"She's taking you to the cleaners," Leandro added with quite a relish.

It would serve you right if I took you to the cleaners.

The shock on Luca's face deepened his brother's smile. "Her exact words. She wants a huge divorce settlement."

Divorce? She was talking divorce? Had she decided he wasn't worth it, after all?

Luca's heart sank like a stone, leaving a gaping void in his chest. Had he self-destructed, then? Had he become that self-fulfilling prophecy? Had he lost the one woman who'd loved him despite the fact that he hadn't deserved it? And he couldn't blame it on what Enzo had passed on to him. No, this was all his doing.

Merda, was it all over already?

"I told you to give her my share of the Conti stock," he offered numbly. Suddenly, his world felt emptier than it had ever been before.

This blackness, this yawning stretch in front of him, this was what would break him. His love for Sophia, that was the only thing that would knock him out at the knees, he realized now. Not some pre-decided genetic sequence. Not a lack of control.

Living without Sophia's love, returning to the meaningless, empty tomb of his life, would send him to madness.

"To quote, 'It costs him nothing to give it away, that bloody stock.' She doesn't want it, Luca." When Luca glared at him, Leandro shrugged again. "Don't shoot the messenger. You left me here to deal with her and she is on a warpath. She wants your personal fortune, your studio, even your countless pianos. Apparently, everything you have ever hidden, everything you have ever made through your *genius*, she wants it. And your antics all over Europe with all those women, you have given her lawyers enough rope to hang you with."

Why say no to CLG stock when it would give her a seat on the most powerful board in Milan? When it would mean the culmination of all her dreams?

She had him utterly baffled, more than a little disconcerted, and he was supposed to be the genius. *Did she hate him so much, then?*

He hadn't left her any other choice when he had left Milan in the dark of night, when he'd made sure tales of his escapades had reached every big media outlet that had chased him. His cruelty haunted him now.

Dio, what had he done?

Leandro wasn't quite finished.

"She has discovered, *to her delight*, her words again, that you're a millionaire a hundred times over. 'Your dear brother is full of little secrets, isn't he?' Her lawyers are quoting 'emotional distress, spousal abuse and abandonment of marriage' as grounds for divorce. Even society's sympathy lies with her. Sophia Rossi is not only clever, she's extremely resourceful."

"What the hell do you mean *society*? This is between me and her."

"No, it's not. It is a scandal now, another Conti spectacle like the last one…like Enzo started. Alex and I can't step out without being hunted by the media. Sophia and Salvatore are talking about *your separation* to everyone who will listen. There was a featured article last week that hinted you were the mastermind behind the innovative waterproof sole technology we use in Conti pumps and those gravity-defying metallic stilettos that made us big globally."

"Huang?" Luca said. "She spoke to Huang."

Leandro nodded. "They are all speculating what you've been up to all these years to have made so much money. They are all questioning your behavior all these years, wondering if you're like Enzo. She made you a person of interest to every rabid newspaper, every network station. I… I can't control what they get their hands on, Luca."

Wave after wave of shock barreled at Luca. Now he understood the gravity in his brother's voice, the concern in those gray eyes.

If someone found out about his birth, if they knew that the same hungry cavern dwelled in his mind, too, the same fear and distaste he saw in Antonio's face would appear in everyone's…

He put his head in his hands, his breath sawing through his throat. Was this all just to hurt him as he had hurt her? Would she reveal the circumstances of his birth, too? Would she make the world think him a shame, as he'd thought of himself for so long? Would she—

"*She is outing me.* She's telling the world who I am," he said, his stomach clenched so hard he couldn't breathe.

Leandro finally leaned back in his chair. "I believe so. Nothing I could say would convince her otherwise."

Luca groaned, the sound coming from the depths of his soul. The groan morphed into laughter that made his lungs burn. He felt like he was caught by an eddy, tossed around this way and that. He laughed until there were tears in his eyes and he was shaking, shivering with relief, with the release of fear and so much love that he couldn't even breathe.

Hands on his temples, he ducked his head, waiting for the dizziness to abate. Tears poured down his cheeks, and he wiped them with shaking fingers.

With his breath returned the image of Sophia that had tormented him for months.

Sophia with her heart in her eyes, her body shaking violently as she kissed him and told him that she accepted all of him. That all he needed to do was give them a chance, a real one.

Sophia, who would not take defeat lying down. Sophia, who fought to the last breath for the people she loved. "Please tell me you did not threaten or manipulate my wife in any way?"

Something flashed in Leandro's gaze. Leandro seemed to have frozen as if he could not believe it. As if it was impossible that Luca had finally, irrevocably fallen in love. "She has also already turned around Rossi's stock. According to some of my sources—"

"Your sources?" Luca demanded. "You are having her watched? Guarding your company?"

"I was worried about her, Luca. So is Salvatore. She works like a demon, she… The news about you that has reached us, she…she has not been the same. Salvatore appointed her CEO of Rossi Leather.

"Her idea for a flagship design store in the midst of Milan's fashion district made the CLG board salivate. The store will display every new product line weeks before they actually hit the market. It will become the center of every designer event in the city. But she fought for her stepfather like a lioness, said it was her family's legacy and they finally voted to call it *Casa Rossi*. Ten designer brands, including Maserati, are going to be part of her inaugural event tomorrow night."

Despite fear beating a tattoo in his blood, Luca nodded. He had no idea if Sophia would take him back, but he meant to spend the rest of his life begging, hounding her, chasing her, generally turning her life upside down. Like she had done with him. If he had to spend the rest of it on his knees, naked and shivering, he would do it.

If he had to spend the next hundred years waiting for her forgiveness and her love, he'd do it happily.

"I have never met a woman quite so ferocious," Tina added with no little pride in her voice.

Ferocious and funny and far too softhearted, the woman he'd fallen in love with was too good for him. "You take her side over your gorgeous brother's?" Luca threw at Tina.

"Since I have discovered that my brother is a donkey's behind, *si*." Tina waited for Leandro to stop laughing, a serious light in her eyes. "Since she has done me the favor of telling me the truth. Since she's the only one who treats me as a grown-up woman and not a commodity to be protected or controlled. Or used as a bargaining chip in blackmail."

Instantly, all humor evaporated from the air. Tension rippled across his shoulders and he saw the same in Leandro's face. Anguish danced in his brother's face and for his sake, Luca hoped Tina would forgive Leandro.

She threw the last words viciously at Antonio, her voice breaking. Antonio, whom Tina had loved so unconditionally, had the grace to look ashamed.

"What truth?" Luca finally managed to say. It seemed Sophia had left no stone unturned in opening their family's vault of secrets.

"That I am not a Conti. That my father was a poor chauffeur *Mama* fell in love with after she left you and Leandro. That my older brother, the Conti Saint, set up my marriage to Kairos because he thought I would fall apart if the truth ever came out and a powerful, handsome husband could make up for it. That my second brother, the Conti Devil, married her to keep my power-hungry husband from breaking my heart. I think I prefer your way, Luca. If I had to choose between one of you manipulating my life as if it were a chess board."

"Tina, *tesoro*, I'm so—"

Tears rolled down Tina's cheeks as she cut off Leandro. "I'm not angry, Leandro. At least not anymore, now that I have had time to recover from the shock. All you and Luca have ever done is love me, *si*? You could have hated me for *Mama*'s abandoning of you. You could have left me to my own fate when she died.

I am your sister and nothing could change that. But I look at Sophia, I look at the state of my marriage, and I realize what a naive fool I am. I am leaving Kairos. And Milan." *She was leaving them both.*

Luca reached her the same time Leandro did. He held her tight while she sobbed. Luca had never been more proud of his little sister.

Fear danced in Leandro's eyes, and Luca shook his head in warning. His brother's job for years had been to protect Luca and Tina. But it was Tina's life now.

Luca kissed her cheek while Leandro compulsively said, "Where are you going? Will you stay with friends? You will tell us if you need help, *si*?"

Tina laughed at Leandro and hugged him tight. "I am an adult, Leandro. I can take care of myself. You're to stay out of this thing between Kairos and me. But *si*, I will keep in touch, although only if you tell me what state Sophia leaves Luca in when she's through with him."

A weight lifted from Luca's chest and he hoped Tina would find happiness in her new journey. He found himself frantically praying to a God he had only ever hated before.

"You're a genius, *si*?" she said to him, exaggerated doubt in her teasing tone.

Luca nodded.

"Then, *per piacere*, do not lose the most wonderful thing to ever happen to you."

Casa Rossi, the first major designer store of Rossi's after its reinvention and the lounge bar on Piazza San

Fedele, glittered on its opening night. Creamy white carpet and sofas, with different designer pieces from every noted brand on the shelves, made the space an intimate, exclusive event.

Pink champagne flowed freely, designer-clad men and women walked around and talked and got noticed by people they wanted to be seen by. More than a few people had approached her. Sophia had no doubt it was more to feed their own curiosity than anything else.

Because she'd dragged the venerable Contis into an out-and-out war. She refused to let Luca hide. She had been terrified when Leandro had come to see her but refused to back down.

Already the list of people who wanted to be invited to the next event was growing exponentially according to her assistant. Sophia had quickly looked through and struck off some of the men who'd called her quite a range of names over the past few years.

She adjusted a buttery-soft white leather clutch, still amazed at the success of her idea. Where Conti Luxury Goods entered, the entire range of companies who had once turned away from Rossi's joined in. The gray wolves were all walking behind her now, like domesticated dogs, following the line of meat to Rossi's.

Luca would so totally get that, she realized with a laugh. She'd have to tell him and then they would make fun of... And just like that, the painful knot in her stomach returned.

Two months since that night. She'd been pitied, smirked at, laughed at, that she had thought herself good enough to take on the Conti Devil. She'd turned her very life into a circus, herself into a cheap act for him. To make their marriage, its failure and Luca the focus of every rabid gossip in Milan.

Already, so many things had come out about him. Luca had to face himself. Accept himself. Only then was there a chance for them…

Having given up even a pretense of pride, which was all she had these days after making such a thoroughly public and humiliating spectacle of herself, of manipulating everything to lure him out, she'd begged Tina to tell her if she'd heard anything from him.

Hysterical that their fates had reversed. Now Tina was the stronger one, the one who told Sophia her brother wasn't worth it while Sophia became a shadow of herself.

She lay awake at night, aching in mind and body, worked like a demon during the day…and it was taking its toll on her. This…faith in him, in her, in their love, the laughter they'd shared, it was burning out now.

What was she going to do if he never returned?

And then she heard it, the soft strains of music coming from the lounge bar beyond the foyer. It had a piano but she had actively looked away from it, for it had the power to send her to her knees now.

This was what he'd made of her. She, who had never been afraid of anything, was now scared of pianos, and music, bikes, the streets leading to the Piazza del Duomo, and couldn't look at chocolate truffles without breaking down into sobs.

Suddenly, a strange silence replaced the soft chatter.

And in that silence came that music again, the point in that vicious circle where it was trapped. Sophia felt like she was living the song.

Heart in her throat, she walked to the lounge.

There he was. He sat at the piano, his head bowed, his fingers flying over it. White shirt and dark trousers, hair wet and gleaming, shoulders fluid. Soft pink light filled the room, casting flashes of light on him. Teasing and taunting her. Driving her utterly mad.

Sophia blinked.

It had to be one of her feverish dreams in which she heard that tune again and again, in which she saw him look at her with that hunger and desire, in which she felt his hands on her, holding her, touching her, driving her out of her own skin. In which she saw him poised over her wet sex, his expression one of utter reverence and wicked desire.

She could feel him between her legs now and she clutched her legs closed tighter.

Her heart thumped. Her breath stuttered. She felt feverish. Tears threatened to spill over. She leaned against the far wall and closed her eyes. She was so cold, exhausted. Like she was breaking apart again and again.

And then the tune rose to its pinnacle, hope and life twisting together.

"Stop, please," she yelled. It did.

A frisson went through her and then she felt him in front of her.

His warmth. The scent of his skin. The air charging around him.

Her eyes flicked open.

Dark shadows under jet-black eyes. Wide, wicked, sensually carved mouth. Blades of cheekbones. Perfectly symmetric planes of his face.

The most beautiful man she had ever seen.

The man she loved beyond bearing.

She extended her arm, fluttered her fingers over his cheek. Ran her thumb over the sweep of one cheekbone and then over the defined curve of his upper lip. Her fingers kept sliding away from his face, so violently was she shaking. She felt his fingers clamp her wrist and hold her hand there against him, leaning into his touch.

She felt the pulse in his neck against her hand, frantic and hurried.

She felt his breath on the back of her palm, frenzied and rough, as if he had run a great distance to find her, instead of prowling from one corner of the room to the other.

She felt him, all of him and she shuddered violently. Her heart slammed against her rib cage.

He *was* standing before her. He was finally here. He had returned.

Sophia drew her hand back and slapped him across the cheek. So hard that his sculpted jaw went back and shock jarred up her arm. The sound of it reverberated in the silence, propelling her out of her nightmarish state. "Leave me alone," she whispered, her voice on the verge of breaking.

He didn't move. Didn't utter a word.

Only gazed at her with glittering eyes. Even in the

pink light, Sophia could see the mark she'd left on his cheek. Desperate, panicky, words came and fell away from her lips.

Please stay. Please want me. Please love me.

Please don't ever leave me like that again.

No, she wouldn't beg.

She made to push away from him but he moved faster. Trapped her against the wall, his arms bracketing her on either side. He said nothing, though, only stared at her, held her like that as if he was completely complacent in that position. As if he was content to hold her in place and gaze at her for eternity.

She kept her gaze at some far point in the distance. If she stared into those eyes, she would break permanently.

"Will you not look at me, Sophia?"

"I hate you. I…despise you. You…are exactly what I always thought you were," she spat at him, her dignity, her self-respect, everything in tatters. Her strength nothing but a shadow in the face of her love for him. "A heartless bastard who can see nothing past his own bloody genius, nothing past his own demons. You were partying with your…damn groupies while I…I…" And then she fell against him, hate and love inseparably twining into a rope, binding him to her. "If you kissed a single one of them, Luca, if you have even touched one with a long pole… I'll kill you with my bare hands." Only then did she raise her eyes. He had never lied to her, but this… She needed to see the answer for herself. "If you so much as… This is over. We are over."

"*Non, cara mia.* I couldn't even look at another woman. I…was a bastard. For those first couple of weeks, I wanted to make sure you hated me. Your words that night, they haunted me. They hurt me. They mocked me. I thought I would give you all the reasons in the world to hate me. I thought I would shake that resolve in your eyes, show you what I truly was.

"But, *Dio*, I couldn't go through with any of it. For the first time in my life, I realized what I had lost and that it had nothing to do with being my father's son. That it was *I* that was ruining my life with my own actions. I promise, *cara*, I could not look at another woman but you."

Something small and tenuous built inside Sophia again. Hope had never terrified her like that. "I did hate you. But I couldn't shake off that faith in us. Is that what love is? This blind, illogical, irrational faith in the man who tears you apart so recklessly when all you've done is love him? I have no more, Luca. I'm done loving you."

He shuddered around her, like a flash of lightning in the sky. His lean body jerked and settled around her again. "You did all this to make me face myself. You would give up on me now?"

She felt his hands move through her hair, his nose buried in it, her name a mantra on his lips. He held her gently as she sobbed her heart out. Two months of tears, two months of fears…two months of staying strong for him. "Sometimes, I feel like you have taken everything from me. Like a bus carried me away from everything that I loved. Like I will never breathe properly again. Like I will never be free again.

"I hate being in love. So much. I… It hurts so much."

"Shh…*tesoro mio*. Shhh…please, Sophia. No more. I can't stand the sound of you crying." She heard the tension rise in him, too, heard the catch in his voice as if he, too, was breaking down.

He pushed away her hair from her forehead, wiped the remaining tears from her cheeks. Gently, oh, so tenderly. "I…ran so far, so fast, that night. But you… you were already a part of me. You… Everything was so colorless, Sophia. Even music could not soothe me. And then I saw myself. As you saw me. And I realized this life that has brought me to you, I could never hate it. *Ti amo, tesoro*. With every breath in me. Will you let me love you, Sophia? Will you give me the chance to be the man you deserve? I swear, *cara mia*, I will never hurt you again."

Sophia threw her arms around his neck and held him tight. Breathed in the scent of him. He was solid and male around her. "Yes, please, Luca. Love me. Spend eternity with me." He breathed a sigh, relief maybe, and held her tightly back. She gave herself over to Luca's love. Her heart was his already.

EPILOGUE

Three years later

"I'VE BROUGHT SOMEONE to see you, Mrs. Conti."

Sophia whirled around at that voice so fast that her head spun, her heart climbed up into her throat. She had seen them only this morning before she left for work, but her heart still ran away from her at the sight of them.

It was only three weeks since she'd returned to work after a six month maternity leave. But she missed spending those lazy mornings in bed when Luca would bring their bawling bundle into their bedroom and all three of them would cuddle, play and sometimes just fall into exhausted sleep after a cranky night.

Luca stood at the door, with the baby basket in hand, wicked mouth curved wide in a smile.

Her assistant, Margie, was faster than Sophia in reaching the new arrivals. She took the precious bundle instantly away from his father and cooed over him, before Sophia had even managed to breathe normally. "You're lucky, Mrs. Conti," Margie said in between the baby gibberish she spouted to their seven-month-old son. "You've got the two most gorgeous men in Italy chained to you."

Sophia looked at her beaming son, gave him a cuddle and a quick kiss before Margie stole him away from her again. "I do, don't I?" Laughing, Sophia met Luca's gaze.

White shirt and blue jeans hugged her husband's lean figure. Blue, ever-present shadows under his eyes. Stubble on his jaw, because he wouldn't have found time this morning to shave. He looked thoroughly disreputable, for once, the very image of the crazy genius he was, and heartbreakingly gorgeous.

"You left without saying goodbye this morning."

Her heart still racing, Sophia sighed. "You looked dead to the world." She knew how little sleep he managed.

"Yes, but I don't like you leaving for the day without kissing me goodbye."

Reaching Luca, she threw her hands around him while he took her mouth in a fast, scorching kiss full of frantic hunger. The same desire flooded her limbs and all she wanted was to steal away with her man for an afternoon of pulse-pounding sex, like they hadn't indulged in a while. Her sensitive nipples peaked when he stroked inside her mouth with erotic expertise that to this day stole her breath. That made her want to be just this wanton creature who made the sexiest man rock hard, and forget all her other roles—daughter, aunt, CEO of a multinational company and even a mother.

Pulling back slowly, he sank his fingers into her hair. Eyes glittered full of wicked invitation. "Take the afternoon off," he said, mirroring her very thought.

Sophia kissed him and drew back quickly before he could ensnare her again. "Even if I did, what about your son? He gets crankiest before his afternoon nap, remember? Takes after his father, the devil."

"He's an angel. Just look at him."

Dark-eyed, dark-haired, with a charming toothless grin, Leo was a mirror image of his father. The look in Luca's eyes when he had held their son for the first time had almost crushed Sophia's heart.

There had been fear, and wonder and hope and so much love. He had lifted the squalling infant in his arms so tenderly, tears running down his cheeks. And then he'd met her gaze. "He looks like me," he'd said then, a sort of helplessness in his voice. As if it broke his heart a little, all over again. "*Dio*, Sophia, what if he…he is like me, too?"

Luca's scars had healed, but not vanished.

Sophia had been crying, too. But she had stayed strong for him. She'd clutched Luca's free hand with hers and squeezed tight. "Does it matter who he looks like when we love him so much? He's a piece of our hearts, isn't he?"

It had taken them only twenty-four hours, however, to realize their son, notwithstanding his cherubic looks, had the temper of the very devil. Within two days he'd reduced Sophia to hysteric tears and a dark fear that she couldn't even calm her own son.

Packing them into his Maserati, Luca had driven

them around all night, lulling them both into frantic sleep. The next night it had begun all over again. Until Luca had started playing the piano.

Only those two things calmed Leo enough to sleep every night now.

The smallest disruption to his schedule, and Leo was known to scream at decibel levels that could rupture unsuspecting eardrums. A thing that seemed to endlessly amuse his two cousins, the perfect little girls they were. "Why couldn't I have a beautiful little doll like Izzie or Chiara?"

His arms around her, Luca nuzzled her neck. "You know what we could do if you want a girl, *cara mia*."

Sophia snorted. "No way. I haven't even lost half the weight I've gained. I wish men gained weight when their wives got pregnant. It's not fair that you...you continue looking like you do while I look like a baby elephant."

"Watch that mouth. That's my lovely wife you're talking about." He pressed a kiss to her temple, reverent and tender. "I love you just as you are, Sophia. I wouldn't change a single thing about you. I would change everything about my past, everything about myself, to prove it, if I could."

The regret and pain in his tone was like a lash against her skin.

He accepted her for everything she was, flaws and all those little eccentricities, and she loved him, too. That she'd hinted, even unknowingly, at denying him that same acceptance was anathema to her.

"Si," Sophia whispered urgently. A shiver went

through her and he held her tighter. "I do. And I trust you, Luca."

Even to this day, she woke up sometimes in the middle of the night, saw him next to her on the bed, usually hogging all the sheets and pushing her to the edge of the bed in his need to hold her tight, and wondered at how much this gorgeous, beautiful man loved her.

And how deeply and how completely. The wonder in his eyes when he looked at Leo and her every day, it humbled her.

"Did you really want a girl, Sophia?"

Sophia locked her hands on top of his, settling into his arms. "Not really. Although I do worry sometimes."

"About what?"

"I think of the future, and I'm sure I'll dread mornings where I have to leave you two at home and walk away. I imagine coming home to a disaster zone."

"Are you saying I'm going to spoil our son?"

"I know you're going to spoil him rotten. And I'll have to be the strict one."

He nipped at her shoulder, his lowered voice a caress. "But you do strict so well, *bella mia*."

Melting on the floor of her office was not an option so Sophia snorted instead. "I see that you're not even saying no."

His hands tightened around her waist, pressing her into his front. The length of his erection was a brand against her back. Her mouth dried, a rush of wetness pooling at her sex.

Sophia caught the moan in her throat, thanking Margie for discreetly walking away with their son to her private sitting area.

In the short time she'd been back at work, Luca and Leo's visits to her workplace were already the highlight of the day for all the women in the office. Everyone wanted to hold her son, and everyone wanted to see Luca—the infamous playboy turned devoted husband and doting, stay-at-home dad—tease, taunt and make their strict boss blush. Or so Margie had told her when Sophia had asked why there was always a rush on their floor during lunchtime.

"I have asked Alex if she'd watch Leo tonight," he said now, swiping that clever tongue over the very spot he had dug his teeth into at the crook of her neck. "She said yes. She also said she was surprised that it had taken us this long to ask her. She *also, also* said she would be keeping tabs, that the minute she hears that Leo's sleeping better, she expects us to take Izzie and Chiara. Even if we have to rip away the little one from my brother's hands."

Sophia laughed. Leandro was so protective of the girls that it took all of Alex's energy to ensure they had the freedom that little girls needed to run around and express themselves.

On the opposite end of the spectrum was her husband, who praised their little boy for his perfect aim when he threw his bowl of mashed peas across the room like it was a soccer ball. Luca had converted a whole room in his studio into a kid-safe playroom for

Leo, who even as a seven-month-old challenged himself into how destructive he could get each day.

"The whole night? Is he ready for it, do you think?"

His fingers laced with hers, he held her tightly. "He is. Are you?"

It was both alarming and a little guilt-inducing to see how easily Luca had taken to fatherhood. He loved doing everything from morning to night without a single complaint. His energy, it seemed, was boundless.

He had watched Leo the whole night for weeks, only bringing him to Sophia for feeding. While Sophia had struggled, Luca had decided it was the perfect cure for his insomnia.

"I know that right now, you know more about his habits than I do, but I thought maybe—"

"Shhh, *bella*. Didn't we talk about this? You've got nothing to feel guilty about. I love looking after him. I love bringing him to visit you here. I love seeing the glow you get when you work your ass off and you make a win in this world. This is our family, Sophia. Our life. This is what works for us. You've worked so hard to get here and it's not like I'm ever going to work a nine-to-five job."

"Yes, but I'm worried that you're not getting any time to yourself. And that you'll probably resent me sometime in the future, or think I'm not—"

"I love you. All of you. The woman who bawled like a baby when she held our son the first time, the woman who told her stepfather, in an uncompromising tone, that she and only she, could run Rossi's the best, the woman who resurrected Rossi's from its broken state, the woman who fought for me like a lioness, the woman who cries every time I play the piano.

"And that woman, that is who I fell in love with. That is who made me see a future full of love. Don't you dare change on me now, *cara mia*.

"I'm aware every minute of every day that I have this happiness, this love, this family with you and Leo because you're who you are. I adore you, *cara mia*, more every day."

Tears pricked at Sophia's eyes, a lump in her throat blocking any words from coming out. Even if she was capable of them with her heart swelling in her chest. She turned and buried her face in his chest.

God, she loved him more and more each day, too. And sometimes, the depth of that love, the power it gave him over her, the possibility of her entire life falling apart at his hands…it choked her, too. That fear was becoming less frequent, though.

When Luca loved, as she'd learned in the last three years, it was with such unerring devotion, it was with such absolute giving, that it filled her with awe.

She squeezed him for all she was worth. "Okay, you and your son have to get out of here if I'm going to take the afternoon off."

Desire glinted in his eyes. *"Si?"*

"Yes, but not for what you're thinking."

"What, then?"

"Shopping," she whispered against his mouth. She stroked her tongue into his mouth and pressed herself against him. His erection was a long, hard length against her belly. Darts of desire shot straight down to her pelvis. "I need new lingerie. Lots of red and black lace, I'm thinking, and those stilettos that I hear are new in the market."

He groaned and leaned his forehead against hers. He was breathing hard as if he'd run a mile. "I guess I should shave, then."

She ran a hand over his jaw, loving the bristly texture against her palm. "No, no shave," she whispered at his ear. Laughing, he hugged her one more time and Sophia thought life couldn't get any better.

* * * * *

In case you missed it, book one in
the LEGENDARY CONTI BROTHERS *duet*
THE SURPRISE CONTI CHILD
is available now!

Uncover the wealthy Di Sione family's sensational
secrets in brand-new eight book series
THE BILLIONAIRE'S LEGACY beginning with
DI SIONE'S INNOCENT CONQUEST
by Carol Marinelli
Also available this month

Turn the page for an exclusive extract of
SLEEPLESS IN MANHATTAN
the first book in USA TODAY *bestselling author*
Sarah Morgan's enthralling new trilogy,
FROM MANHATTAN WITH LOVE*!*

PAIGE STOOD FOR a moment, thinking how unpredictable life was.

Who would have thought that herself, Eva and Frankie losing their jobs would have turned out so well?

Urban Genie existed only because life had laid a twist in her path.

Change had been forced on her, but it had proved to be a good thing.

Instead of fighting it, she should embrace it.

What had Jake said?

Sometimes you have to let life happen.

Maybe she should try to do that a bit more.

And maybe one day she'd look back and realize that *not* being with Jake was the best thing that could have happened—because if she'd been with Jake she wouldn't have met—

Whom?

Would she ever meet someone who made her feel the way Jake did?

She stood leaning on the railing, gazing at the city she loved.

The lights of Manhattan sparkled like a thousand stars against a midnight sky and now, finally, as the last of the guests made their way to the elevators, she allowed herself a moment to enjoy it.

"Time to relax and celebrate, I think."

Jake's voice came from behind her and she turned to find him holding two glasses of champagne. He handed her one. "To Urban Genie."

"I don't drink while I'm working." And while Jake was present this was definitely still work.

She knew better than to lower her guard a second time.

"The guests have gone. You're no longer working. Your job is done."

"I'm not off duty until the clear-up has finished." And then tomorrow would be the follow-up, the post-mortem. Discussions on what they might have done differently. They'd unpick every part of the event and put it back together again. By the time they'd finished they'd have found every weak spot and strengthened it.

"I don't think one glass of champagne is going to impair your ability to supervise that. Congratulations." He tapped his glass against hers. "Spectacular. Any new business leads?"

"Plenty. First up is a baby shower next week. Not much time to prepare, but it's a good event."

He winced. "A baby shower is *good*?"

"Yes. Partly because the woman throwing it for her

pregnant colleague is CEO of a fashion importer. But all business is good."

"Chase Adams is impressed. By tomorrow word will have got around that Urban Genie is the best event concierge company in Manhattan. Prepare to be busy."

"I'm prepared."

His praise warmed her. Her heart lifted.

He stood next to her and the brush of his sleeve against her bare arm made her shiver.

His gaze collided briefly with hers and she thought she saw a blaze of heat, but then he looked away and she did, too, her face burning.

She was doing it again. Imagining things.

And it had to stop.

It had to stop right now.

No more embarrassing herself. No more embarrassing *him*.

She turned her head to look at him but he was staring straight ahead, his handsome face blank of expression.

"Thank you," she said.

"For what?"

"For asking us to do this. For giving us free rein and no budget. For trusting us. For inviting influential people and decision-makers. For making Urban Genie happen." She realized how much she owed him. "I hate accepting help—"

"I know, but that isn't what happened here. You did it yourself, Paige."

"But I wouldn't have been able to do it without you. I'm grateful. If you hadn't suggested it, pushed

me that night on the terrace, I wouldn't have done it."
She breathed in. Now was as good a time as any to
say everything that needed to be said. And if she said
it aloud maybe it would help both of them. "There's
something else—" She saw him tense and felt a flash
of guilt that he felt the need to be defensive around her.
Definitely time to clear the air. "I owe you an apology."

"For what?"

"For misreading the situation the other night. For
making things awkward between us. I was…" She
hesitated, trying to find the right words. "I guess you
could say I was doing an Eva. I was looking for things
that weren't there. I was close to panic and you were
trying to distract me. I understand that now. I don't
want you feeling that you have to avoid me, or be careful around me. I'd never want that. I—"

"Don't. Don't apologize."

He gripped the railing and she noticed his knuckles were white.

"I wanted to clear it up, that's all. It was a kiss.
Didn't mean anything. Two people trapped in an elevator, one of whom was feeling vulnerable." *Shut up
right now, Paige.* "I know I'm not your type. I know
you don't have those feelings. I'm like your little sister. I get that. So—"

"Oh, for— *Seriously?*" He interrupted her with a
low growl and finally turned to face her. "After what
happened the other night you really think I see you as
a little sister? You think I could kiss you that way if I
felt like that about you?"

She stared at him, her heart drumming a rhythm

against her chest. "I thought— You said— I thought you saw me that way."

"Yeah, well, I tried." He gave a humorless laugh and drained his champagne in one mouthful. "God knows, I tried. I've done everything short of asking Matt for a baby photo of you and sticking that to my wall. Nothing works. And do you know why? Because I *do* have feelings, you're *not* little and you're not my damn *sister*."

Shock struck her like a bolt of lightning.

They were the only two people left on the terrace. Just them and the Manhattan night. The buildings rose around them—dark shapes enveloping them in intimate shadows and the shimmer of light.

The storm clouds were gathering, creating ominous shadows in the dark sky.

The sudden lick of wind held the promise of rain.

Paige was oblivious. The sky might have come crashing down and she wouldn't have noticed.

Her mouth was so dry she could hardly form the words. "But if you feel that way, if you do have feelings, why do you keep saying—" She stumbled over the words, confused. "Why haven't you ever done anything about it?"

"Why do you think?"

There was a cynical, bitter edge to Jake's tone that didn't fit the nature of their conversation. None of the pieces fitted. She couldn't think. Everything about her had ceased to function.

"Because of Matt?"

"Partly. He'd kick my butt. And I wouldn't blame

him." He stared down at his hands, as if they were something that didn't belong to him. As if he was worried about what they might do.

"Because you're not interested in relationships—or 'complications,' as you call them?"

"Exactly."

"But sex doesn't have to be a relationship. It can just be sex. You said so yourself."

"Not with you."

His tone was harsh and she took a step back, shocked. They'd often argued, baited each other, but she'd never heard that edge of steel in his voice before.

"Why? What's different about me?"

"I'm not going to screw you and walk away, Paige. That's not going to happen."

"Because of our friendship? Because you're worried it would be awkward?"

"Yeah, that, too."

"Too? What else?" She stared at him, bemused.

He was silent.

"Jake? What else?"

He swore under his breath. "Because I care about you. I don't want to hurt you. There's already been enough damage to your heart. You don't need more."

The first raindrops started to fall.

Paige was still oblivious.

Her head spun with questions. *Where? What? Why? How much?* "So you— Wait—" She struggled to make sense of it. "You're saying that you've been *protecting* me? No. That can't be true. You're the only one who *doesn't* protect me. When everyone else is wrapping me in cotton wool, you handle me as though you're throwing the first pitch at a game."

He didn't protect her. He *didn't*. Not Jake.

She waited for him to agree with her, to confirm that he didn't protect her.

He was silent.

There was a throbbing in her head. She lifted her fingers to her forehead and rubbed. The storm was closing in—she could feel it. And not just in the sky above her.

"I *know* you don't protect me." She tried to focus, tried to examine the information and shook her head. "Just the other night, when we found out we'd lost our jobs, Matt was sympathetic but you were brutal. I was ready to cry, but you made me so *angry* and—" She stared at him, understanding. She felt the color drain from her face. "You did it on purpose. You made me angry on purpose."

"You get more done when you're angry," he said flatly. "And you needed to get things done."

No denial.

He'd goaded her. Galvanized her into action.

"You challenge every idea I have." She felt dizzy. "We fight. All the time. If I say something is black, you say it's white."

He stood in silence, not bothering to deny it, and she shook her head in disbelief.

"You *make* me angry. You do that on purpose. Because if I'm angry with you, then I'm not—" She'd been blind. She breathed hard, adjusting to this new picture of their relationship. The first boom of thunder split the air but she ignored it. "How long? How long, Jake?"

"How long, what?" He yanked at his bow tie with impatient fingers.

His gaze shifted from hers. He looked like a man who wanted to be anywhere but with her.

"How long have you cared? How long have you been p-protecting me?" She stumbled over the word— and the thought.

He ran his hand over his jaw. "Since I walked through the door of that damn hospital room and saw you sitting on the bed in your Snoopy T-shirt, with that enormous smile on your face. You were so brave. The most frightened brave person I'd ever seen. And you tried so hard not to let anyone see it. I have *always* protected you, Paige. Except for the other night, when I let my guard down."

But he'd been protecting her then, too. He'd been taking care of her when she'd been so terrified she hadn't known what to do.

"So you thought I was brave, but not strong? Not strong enough to cope alone without protection? I don't understand. I thought you weren't interested, that you didn't want this, and now I discover—" It was a struggle to process it. "So this whole time you *did* care about me. You *do*."

Rain was falling steadily now, landing in droplets on his jacket and her hair.

"Paige—"

"The kiss the other night—"

"Was a mistake."

"But it was real. It wasn't because I was a pair of red lips in an elevator. All these days, months, *years* I've been telling myself you didn't feel anything. All the time I've been confused because my instincts were so wrong and I couldn't understand why. But now I do. They weren't wrong. *I* wasn't wrong."

"Maybe you weren't."

"So why let me think that?"

"Because it was easier."

"Easier than what? Telling me the truth? News flash—and, by the way, I thought you knew this— I don't want to be protected. I want to live my life. You're the one who's always telling me to take more risks."

"Yeah, well, that proves you shouldn't listen to anything I tell you. We should go inside before you catch pneumonia."

He eased away from the railings and she caught his arm.

"I'll go inside when I decide to go inside." The rain was soaking her skin. "What happens now?"

"Nothing. I know you don't want to be protected but that's tough, Paige, because that's what I'm doing. I'm not what you're looking for and I never have been. We don't want the same thing. There's a car waiting downstairs to take you and the other two home. Make sure you use it."

Without giving her a chance to respond, Jake strode away from her toward the bank of elevators and left her standing there, alone in the glittering cityscape, watching the entire shape of her life change. Another twist. Another turn. The unexpected.

Don't miss SLEEPLESS IN MANHATTAN
by Sarah Morgan,
available from HQN Books.

#3453 MARRYING HER ROYAL ENEMY
Kingdoms & Crowns
by Jennifer Hayward
Most women would kill to be draped in ivory and walking up the aisle toward King Kostas Laskos. But Stella Constantinides naively bared her heart to Kostas to disastrous effect once before and this feisty princess refuses to be his pawn ever again.

#3454 HIS MISTRESS FOR A WEEK
by Melanie Milburne
Years ago, Clementine Scott clashed spectacularly with arrogant architect Alistair Hawthorne and swore she'd never have anything to do with him again! But when Clem's brother disappears with Alistair's stepsister, she's forced to go with Alastair to Monte Carlo to retrieve them!

#3455 IN THE SHEIKH'S SERVICE
by Susan Stephens
Sheikh Shazim Al Q'Aqabi must resist his instant attraction to mysterious dancer Isla Sinclair, for duty is Shazim's only mistress. Until Isla is revealed as the prize winner who will travel to the desert to work with him...making their chemistry impossible to ignore.

#3456 CLAIMING HIS WEDDING NIGHT
by Louise Fuller
Addie Farrell's marriage to casino magnate Malachi King lasted exactly one day, until she discovered their love was a sham. Now Addie must prepare to face her husband—and their dangerously seductive chemistry—once again!

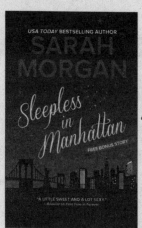

USA TODAY BESTSELLING AUTHOR
SARAH MORGAN

Sleepless in Manhattan

FREE BONUS STORY

"A LITTLE SWEET AND A LOT SEXY."
—*Booklist on First Time in Forever*

$7.99 U.S./$9.99 CAN.

"I came here to set a few things straight with you," Rahim
sneered, deeply resentful that she'd led him to question
himself when there was no doubt where his destiny lay.
"You thought what happened in Dar-Aman wouldn't go
unchallenged. You were wrong."

Allegra's hand jerked to her stomach, her eyes more
vivid against her ashen colour. "No. Please…"

From across the room, Rahim saw her sway. With a
curse, he charged forward and caught her as her legs gave
way. It occurred to him then that she hadn't answered him
when he'd asked what ailed her. Swinging her up into his
arms, he carried her to the sofa and laid her down.

With a low moan, she tried to get up. Rahim stayed her
with a firm hand. "I'm going to get you some water. Then
you'll tell me what's wrong with you. And what the hell
you're doing giving long speeches and photo ops when
you should be in bed."

Her mouth pursed mutinously for a moment before she gave a small nod.

Rising, he crossed to the bar and poured a glass of water. She'd sat up by the time he returned. Silently she took the water and sipped, her wary eyes following him as he sat on the sturdy coffee table directly in front of her.

"Now tell me what's wrong with you."

The sleek knot at her nape had come undone during the journey to the sofa, and twin falls of chocolate-brown hair framed her face as she bent her head. Rahim gritted his teeth against the urge to brush it back, soothe whatever was troubling her, reassure her that he meant her no harm.

He was so busy fighting his baser urges, and sternly reminding himself that he was in the right and she in the wrong, that he didn't hear her whispered words.

"What did you say?"

Her jerky inhale wobbled the glass in her hands. "I said I'm not sick, but I can't go to prison because I'm pregnant." She raised her head then and stared back at him with eyes black with despair. "I'm carrying your child, Rahim."

Don't miss
THE DI SIONE SECRET BABY
by Maya Blake,
available August 2016 wherever
Harlequin Presents® books and ebooks are sold.

www.Harlequin.com